# Freshman

ROXEY B.

ISBN 978-1-0980-7821-8 (paperback)
ISBN 978-1-0980-7822-5 (digital)

Christian Faith Publishing, Inc.
832 Park Avenue
Meadville, PA 16335
www.christianfaithpublishing.com

Printed in the United States of America

To my family with ♥

# CHAPTER 1

AUGUST 27, THE FIRST day of school, wake up out of my queen-size bed with character-print bedding. I wake up to the sunrise smelling the first day of school in the air. I jump out of bed with excitement, already had my clothes picked out the night before—new high-waisted skinny jeans, half-topped shirt that says "Queen" in gold writing and fresh, new white low-top kicks with gold-trim ball on the back-ankle socks. Out my room down the stairs to the kitchen I go. No time really for breakfast, so I grab some pop tarts and chocolate milk and on out the house. To the bus stop, I head with my leather pearl backpack—ready to seize the day, thinking to myself, *One day I won't be riding this huge yellow bus. I will be in a drop top of some kind.*

While waiting at the bus stop who but the one and only shows up—Tyler the genius, betta know as Ty Ty. He is the cutest genus I have ever seen, but I wouldn't let him know that. He shows up with fresh high-top black-and-red kicks, starched jeans, a black shirt with red trim on the short of his sleeves. His braids was always on point; they are just past his shoulders.

"Hey, Carmella," Ty Ty said, "you are looking good as always".

"Hi, Ty, how was your summer?" said Carmella.

"It was great. I went to two different camps. You know, I have to be multitalented, can't have just one," he replied with a smirk on his face. "What did you do this summer?"

"I will tell you all about it later—" Before Carmella could finish her sentence the bus showed up, and they got on.

The bus driver has these long, colorful fingernails, hair in a finger wave better known as a freeze. Chewing on her gum, she says, "Good morning, high schoolers," as she shut the bus door behind us.

We went to our seats—no, we didn't sit together; we are too cool for that. So "Ty" is what I call Tyler because its much cooler than "Ty Ty." He needs to grow out of that name. He sits behind me. On to the next stop, we pick up Lee Lee. Hey, this chick is the business. She gets on the bus and sits right in front of me with her leggings hand printed of every color and a top that flows down to her ankles with slits on the sides. Yes, she is rocking the customized slide in kicks.

"Hey, Mella, wuz cookin'?"

"Nothing much," I said.

"So you know over the summer, I went to nail camp, and I'm going to have your nails, so fly in no time."

Lee Lee does my nails on our way headed to school. They're a white matte with QUEEN on both my ring finger nails, sparkled with gold, of course. As I say, "If it's not gold or rose gold, don't do it." LOL. She finished my nails in the time it takes to get from her stop to school. Wow, that girl is good!

Off the bus, up the stairs to head into school, I looked up at the school name—Royale Technical High. As I'm walking down the hall making my way to homeroom, I'm looking around, taking it all in. The awards the school has won over the years for sports, art, and being one of the top schools in our state.

Oh my, here comes the twins. Now these twins are truly nothing to play around with. They are quiet, but one of those quiets that is very eerie that you kind of stay away from. They both are on the basketball team, they can play too! Been that way since middle school. Shareé is light skinned with long jet-black hair and brown eyes with long eyelashes. She's only five foot six, nice build and straight-up tomboy. Shará is an albino (how cool is that!). She is five foot eight, shaggy, long blondish hair (can we say conditioner), big brown—with a hint of honey-brown flecks—eyes. She could be a model, don't know why she balls, but nowadays, everyone just doesn't want to be the best, but they have to have multiple talents to boot. Shareé always has her hair in a ponytail, and Shará, she is so the female version of Shareé. Today her hair is in a cute messy bun at the top of her head with the rest long past her shoulders. They are both in high-top kicks, and yes, they are customized with their initials on them—all-black high tops with w in turquoise. They both have on gym shorts. Shareé wears those tights under hers. Their t-shirts are turquoise blue. Shareé has a headband on her head. They both have basketballs in their hands. As they are passing, they call out, "Hey, Carmella, how you been, girl?" They didn't even give me a chance to reply; they just kept on walking, mumbling something.

"We don't even really like here like that," Shareé said. Shará came back with, "Yeah, true, but her style stays on point. You have to give her that."

*Homeroom #703.* As I walk in, Joz, the school gossip, is already in the third row, second seat. I think to myself, *I will not sit by her.* She is in a baby-doll dress with thick-soled shoes, popping her bubble gum (ugh!), and her braids, which she has been wearing since the sixth grade. I wonder what her real hair looks like. Her backpack was on the floor by her desk. She is on her phone as always. I sat in the first row, second seat. As I began to sit down, in walks my boy Telion. I called him Teli. We have been cool since, um, yeah, *forever.* His family is government workers, and they have always been located where my parents have—funny coincidence, huh? He came over and sat in the second row, second seat.

"Wuz up, Queen?" Telion says. "Oh, you trying to be funny."

I say with a smile, "No I've always seen you that way. Just was wondering when will you see yourself that way." He always had something to say to make me think, *Oh really.*

Then walks in our homeroom teacher, a short and stout woman. She has on joggers with heels and a shirt with the sleeves cut off and slits on the sides. I'm thinking, *Nice, real nice.*

"Hello, students, this is the first day of school as you all know, and I'm Ms. Winshire, your homeroom teacher. In this class, you will study, do your homework, and—let me speak yawls language—*chill.* Don't go too far with your chillin' 'cause if you don't have something to do, I can always give you something to do. Is that clear?"

Everyone nodded in agreement. For the ones who don't already have their schedule, she printed them off at her computer. At this time…

"Excuse me, young lady," Ms. Winshire said, "who might you be?"

The girl just looked blankly at her. After some seconds go by, she said, "Oh, um, are you talking to me?"

"You are the only one that has walked into my classroom and, might I add, *late!*" said Ms. Winshire.

"My apologies, I'm new here."

"Ain't we all?" said Joz

"I didn't…well, I got lost. Security help me to get here. My name is Mo'Lynn."

"Well, Mo'Lynn, go on and have a seat," said Ms. Winshire

As she was walking to the empty seat on the fourth row, the bell rang. So out of homeroom, everyone dashed through the halls, making sure they are not late to class. Telion says, "Hey, C, you want me to walk you to your next class?" I think to myself, *What a gentleman,* but he doesn't give me the chance to answer. He looks at my schedule and says, "Well, look at that. We are going to the same class."

After first, second, third, and fourth periods, it's finally lunch time. This is where you get to see most of all the freshmen—meet and greet, as the principal calls it.

Lee Lee runs up to me. "Hey, chick, as you know, I have already scooped us a seat. It's where we can see everyone." Lee Lee scored us some really good seat outside on the patio. The first day of school breeze is so nice, the best breeze of new beginnings. We have three booths on the patio—it's Lee Lee (who is crushing on Ty), Teli, the twins, Joz (who is someone you didn't want but you have to have around), and myself.

So we start to get up and peep at the scene; the twins and the boys stay at the booth. Lee Lee, Joz, and I began to walk around just to check things out, see what's happening.

"Why is she over there looking like a lost puppy?" Joz said.

"Who are you referring to?" said Lee Lee with an attitude, because she says and thinks all the time that Joz is so annoying.

"Her."

"Her who?"

"Her from homeroom."

"Can you be clearer, Joz? There are a lot of 'hers' in homeroom."

Joz rolled her eyes and pointed her finger and said, "Her—that Mo'Lynn girl." As they go back and forth, I look in the way Joz is pointing.

"Oh her!" Lee Lee said, laughing.

We began to walk over to her, and Joz, being who she is, says, "Why are you over here looking all ugly. If you want, you can come look ugly with us."

Lee Lee interrupted. "Um, who you are calling ugly? I haven't ever seen that—no, not this one!"

Mo'Lynn looks at us and shrugs her shoulder, says quietly, "Why not?"

We head back to the booth with the twins and the boys.

"Oh, lookie, lookie," Shareé said, "we are picking up strays now?"

"Oh, hush it, sis," Shará says. "I'm Shará. This is my twin, Shareé."

"Um, if she can't tell that, she is either stupid or blind," Shareé said. Everyone laughed. Shará gives Shareé a look, and she chills out only for a moment.

Shará continues. "As I was saying, we are the twins. This is Tyler, also known as Ty Ty."

I stated, "We are in high school now. Call him Tyler or Ty."

"Um, ladies, I can speak for myself. Hey, I'm Tyler, but you can call me Ty." He sticks out his hand to shake Mo'Lynn, who just says hi. Shará keeps talking with her hand; she gestures and say, "This is Telion."

Telion said, "'Sup."

Tyler added, "And you have already met Carmella, Joz, and Lee Lee."

The bell rings, and it's off to fifth, sixth and seventh period. Wow, what a day.

Back on the big yellow bus, Lee Lee gets off first. "Hey, chick, I will either call you or come by, okay?"

"Kool," I said.

She waves as she gets off the bus. "You know I would love to see you later, Tyler." Ty doesn't even look her way or reply.

"Here's our stop, Carmella," Ty said. He walks me to my door. "Hey, what a day, huh?"

"Yeah, it was, but I must say it was kool."

"How do you like the new girl—what's her name?"

"Mo'Lynn? I don't know her to like or not like her."

"Well, that time will come. I will see ya!"

"Okay, Ty."

I walked in the house, threw my backpack on the couch, and yes, my dear ole mother was in the kitchen, whipping something up. My mom is a chef. She is always cooking and trying things out—still looking to one day have her own restaurant. Since dad moves around so much, she is sticking to catering *for now*!

"Here, sweetness, try this and let me know what you think. I'm trying a new recipe."

"Yeah, Má, this is really good! I love your wangs. Is this for dinner?"

"Yes, it is. Grab you a snack for now, then when dad gets home, we will eat."

"Okay," I said. I grabbed me a bar of chocolate and headed up to my room after picking my backpack off the couch.

I entered my room, threw my backpack on the bed, pounced right beside it, said, "Wow, what a day! Everything that should have happened today did."

I got my journal and began to write how my first day of freshman year went—the people I met, the ones I still know, the new teachers, that huge yellow bus that would be picking me up every morning to take me to school right along with my friends, the cafeteria, and the new girl we met. Will she last in our group? Who knows? New beginning, a new place in life to start all over. Leave middle school behind and focus on high school. First day, what a day!

Mom shouts, "Dad's home! Let's eat."

*Well, journal, until next time I write.* I place it back in my desk, head out of my room, and down the stairs I went. "Hello, dear ole dad!"

"Hey, my golden heart! How was your day?"

"It was cool, Daddy. We even met a new girl at school today. She is quite a weird one, but hey, we will see how it goes. How was your day?"

Dad takes off his uniform blouse, as they call it in the military. He is a master sergeant waiting to be promoted. He has also been thinking about retirement. Yeah, I heard him and Mom talking about it. "It was a long day. I had a meeting to go to, then I went and PT'ed with the Marines, went to counselings and now I'm home."

I smiled at my father; he is truly a really great dad. He loves my mom and me; it's unconditional. Even when he is tired, like today, he doesn't want to show it; he still shows his love.

Mom comes in as Dad sits down at the table, and she bends down while holding the wings and kisses Dad on the cheek. "Hey, Big Daddy, you ready to taste something extraordinary?"

"You betta know it, sweet thang. You got it stanking up in here," Dad said. Mom placed the wings on the table with homemade waffle fries, pickles, carrots, and celery sticks, and oh yeah, the homemade tea.

As Mom sits down, we hold hands to say grace. "Lord God, thank you for the food that we are about to receive for the nourishment of our bodies, and please bless all hands in preparation that their hearts, minds, and souls desire to have a deeper walk with you." And we all say "Amen," then we dig in.

I'm the messy eater. I have homemade sauce all over my face and hands, and all you can hear is smacking, no talking—that's how you know it's good. After dinner, I clean the kitchen, and Mom and Dad chill outside on the porch, talking about whatsoever shooting the breeze. I stood in the screen door and thought to myself, *One day, I will have that too.*

I go up to my room, and I have three different messages on my phone.

Lee Lee: HEY CHICK-A-DEE MY APOLOGIES COULDN'T COME BY TODAY IM AT THE SHOPEN WITH MY PARENTS AND OH YEAH I HAVE SOME NEW STYLES AND DESIGNS I WANT TO TRY ON YOUR NAILS SO COME BY THIS SATURDAY.

Joz: YOU ARE SO RUDE WHY DIDN'T YOU REPLY. I WANTED TO TELL YOU ABOUT THE NEWS I FOUND ON THE NEW GIRL. MO'LYNN IF SHE'S GOING TO BE HANGING WITH US, I GOT TO KNOW THE SCOOP. HIT ME BACK GIRL! I WILL NOT BE REPLYING TO HER TONIGHT I WILL SEE HER AT SCHOOL I SAY TO MYSELF.

Ty: HEY JUST WANTED TO SAY IT WAS NICE WALKING YOU HOME.

I sit on my bed and just sigh. *Ty, really*. He is cool and all, but um, too early. I still want to explore and see what's out there. He has been crushing on me since middle school. I throw my phone on the bed and began to look through my clothes to pick out for the rest of the week. I just can't be standing in front of a full, well-organized closet, lying to myself, talking about I don't have nothing to wear. Nope, I'm going to find my clothes for the rest of the school week so that can be one less thing I have to do. After I'm done with that, I shower, chill for a bit, and beddy-bye I go.

It's 6:50 a.m. My alarm clock rings up and at 'em. I go brush my face and wash my teeth. LOL, I mean wash my face and brush my teeth. I have to get this backward talking betta; I'm a high schooler now. That was cute in elementary, then faded in middle school. I look in the mirror at my natural mohawk and say to myself, "Yes, honey, yes." I went to my room to get dressed, head downstairs to grab a pop tart and a chocolate milk, then off to the bus stop. The time to be there is 7:15 a.m. Yeah, I know did all that in twenty-five minutes. I need to wake up earlier—this rushing is not good for a sista, I have to get my eight hours of sleep. If not, it's not good for *no one*!

Ty is already at the bus stop; we smile at each other and get on the bus. Lee Lee's stop, then we are off to school.

"It's Friday, y'all!" Lee Lee says as we get off the bus heading into the school.

"Yelp! First week of school almost ovaaaaaa!" I say with excitement.

"What's your plans for the weekend?" With no pause for an answer, Lee Lee responds to herself, "I will be at the Shopen, then we go to the temple."

Ty says, "I will be hanging out with the boz playing ball, going to the mall, movies, whatever." He shrugs his shoulders.

"Hit me up. I would love to hang with you and the boz are—just you," Lee says, giving Ty the flirty eyes.

"I don't know what I will be doing this weekend," I say after seeing Ty gave no response to Lee's request.

*Homeroom #703.* Before we get in the room good...

"Why you didn't hit me back up last night? I told you I had news," Joz demands to me.

"I just waited until I seen you now. Soooooooooooo, wuz up?"

"Girl, Mo'Lynn lives with her retired grandparents. I wonder why and where is her mother," Joz says nosily.

I snap a bit. "Why you just don't ask her instead of snooping around?"

"Because I report the news. I don't ask unless I have too." Joz pops her gum.

"You mean you report mess?" Lee Lee chuckles.

"You know what?" Joz rolls her eyes.

"Nope. Who is what?" Lee rolls her neck.

"One day, you going to really need my report, messy skills, y'all say." Joz gives us a look.

"Um, huh, and you will let us know too," I say as I look over at Lee.

"Yeah, girl, you know I will," Joz says as she slaps my shoulder and heads to her seat.

Mo'Lynn walks in, heading to the third seat on the fourth row. She was in her jeans hitting right at the ankle, tank with a cami over it; her kicks are purple, which matches her tank. Her permed hair is a shoulder-length bob. She is a simple-looking girl. She is still that weird quiet. Mo'Lynn begin to sit down. Not even two seconds before her biscuits is warm in the seat...

"Um, are you going to speak? You know you see me." Joz was popping her gum.

Mo'Lynn looks at Joz. "Hi."

"Girl, stop with all that shyness. It's not cute." Joz pulls her gum with her fingers.

The bell has rung as Mo'Lynn gathers her books to head out the door.

Lunch time. Lunch time. I'm so hungry. Maybe I need to change my schedule so I can go to lunch earlier. I'm in line, and here comes Teli. "What ya getting?"

I smile. "Hot chips with cheese on top with something to drink."

"You going to share?" Teli ask.

"Maybe," I say.

"I was just kidding with ya, just wanted to see if you would give me some," Teli says while hitting his mitt. They do that when it's tough. They say it's breaking it in ar whatever. So off to the booth we go; the crew is all there.

'Soooooo, Mo', where are you from?" Joz ask.

"You really need to chill off her. Let her scope things out shut, give her some breathing room," Shará says.

"Thank you, but I can speak for myself." Mo' continue as Shará give her a stank look. "Joz, since you are so nosey, I'm from where I'm from, will be where I be, and going where I'm going!" Mo' snaps.

Shareé laughs. "And in that order!" We all join in laughter. Joz looks at us with disgust. She doesn't have a response, so now maybe she will leave Mo' alone, but then again, Mo' might have made it worst.

We eat, laugh, talk about everything and nothing. Then off to class. Lee Lee grabs Mo' shoulder and tells her, "That was a good come back. Keep them coming. You have to stay ready for Joz." Lee Lee winks her left eye. Mo' smiles and walks to her class.

On the bus headed back home, once we reach our stop, Ty says, "Hey, if you want to hang this weekend, just let me know." I smile and just sit on the porch, not ready to go in. I watch him walk down the street headed home until I don't see him. Then I go in the house. Mom is whipping up something again.

"Sweet love, how was school?"

"It was kool. Mo', the new gurl, snapped on Joz."

"Now why would she do that?"

"Má, you know why."

Má looks at me with a blank stare and that one eyebrow raised up.

"'Cause Joz is nosy, always in someone's buziness."

"Oh well, you say she has been that way since you meet her, but you keep her around?" Má questions.

"I like her and all, but…"

Má looks at me with a smile. I began to walk off, and Má stop me in my tracks. "Carmella, we have people coming over this weekend. Saturday night I'm going to host a little get-together. Good food, games, and you can invite your friends if you like."

"Everyone loves your food. What time Saturday?"

"Let's see, 6:00 p.m. until."

"Cool. I will send out a mass text right now."

I sent a message to everyone, GET TOGETHER AT MY HOUSE SAT 6PM-UNTIL. HIT ME BACK IF YOU ARE COMING THROUGH.

Lee Lee: YOU KNOW I'M THERE.

Joz: YELP.

Teli: MOST DEF.

Ty: IF YOUR MOM IS COOKING & YOUR DAD ON THE GRILL YOU KNOW I'M THERE.

Twins: INDEED.

"Carmilla!" Mom calls for me.

"Yes, Má?"

"There is a retired military family that just moved here. I met them at the grocery store today. Sweet people, I invited them over and their granddaughter."

Not really thinking, I said "Okay" and headed up to my room. All man, it just dawned on me. I don't have Mo'Lynn's number to text her about tomorrow. Oh well, maybe Joz will let her know since she is so interested in seeing what Mo'Lynn is about.

# CHAPTER 2

SATURDAY, YES SATURDAY. No school. Chill time until all the people that Mom invited over get here. When Mom do these get-togethers, *they are the buziness*—people always showing up and afterward asking when will the next one be. I always help set up, and yes, I wear my mother's catering shirt. It's black, I don't know why, but it is that says on the top right side of the shirt UMMMMMM, with red rhinestone lips licking. On the back, it says UMMMMMM CATERING SERVICES in white. The menu for the get-together is homemade everything— four different type of wangs, meatballs, Dad's famous beans, small corn on the cob, tattered salad, popsicles, red velvet cupcakes with cream-cheese icing, and sun-brewed tea. Mom loves homemade over anything else. She cooks her food, as she says, with "love, joy, and a sprinkle of grace." Ummm, ummm, ummm!

I head out to the backyard through the kitchen. We sit on about a half of an acre. The backyard has the best green grass you have ever seen with some yellow on its tips. We have lilys and roses growing along the left fence line. There is a bomb firepit that sits smack-dab in the middle of the yard. Dad has his grill set up right on the patio. We also have a fireplace outside on the patio as well. Then we have the lawn furniture, it's a pretty turquoise and brown. When you walk out to the grass, there is a hammock to the right and four wicker chairs that sit around the pit. Mom made them, and Dad helped a little bit. I just watched from time to time. LOL. The yard is mani-cured by Dad, of course.

"Mom, do we have to set out tables and junk? Can we just have chairs everywhere?" I yell from the backyard to the kitchen.

"No, ma'am," Má begins. "Set up a couple of the card tables. People don't want to stand up and eat."

I mumbled to myself, "Well, isn't that what a get-together is— you just eat anywhere?"

The backyard is all set up. I'm back in the kitchen being the taster. Families are starting to show up. Dad welcomes everyone through the back gate. The music is playing, the setup is right, now it's time to have a great time.

"Your mom really can cook. Invite me over anytime." Ty smacks.

I chuckle a bit. "Thanks. I will let Má know."

"Naw, I will tell her 'cause I got to make sure I'm always invited," Ty says as he licks his fingers. I laugh as Ty walks off to go compliment my mom's cooking to her.

I see Mo'Lynn and her grandparents chilling, conversing with my parents. I walk over to them. Mo' is still this quite weird I just can't figure out. After making my plate, I tap her on the shoulder. "Hey, you want to sit at the bomb fire with me?"

"Sure, let me grab some more wangs," Mo' says.

"So how are you liking things so far?" I ask.

"It's cool just like any other place." Mo' picks up a wang.

"What all places have you been?"

"Pretty much here and there." Mo' shrugs her shoulders.

"You really don't talk much or give any real answers, do ya?" I ask.

"Well, there's really not much to tell."

"How long have you been with your grandparents?"

"Since I was three. I don't know my mom. She doesn't come around."

"You haven't seen your mom since you were three? Wow!"

"Right," Mo' says.

"Interesting," I say quizzically.

"Hey, chicks, what's up?" Lee Lee sits in a chair.

"Nothin' much, just chillin', talking about nothin'." I look at Mo'.

"Do I have anything on my face?" Lee Lee asked.

"Why?" I look over. Mo' just looks with a blank stare.

"Because you know who is about to come over." Lee Lee starts to whip nothing from her face.

"You are crushing hard on Ty, and he doesn't see you, like…" I whip my hands on my pants.

"How you know? Tyler told you something?" Lee frowns.

"Nope. It's just when you flirt with him and send your signals, he doesn't pay you no attention." I take a sip of my tea.

"He's just playing hard to get. He mines. He just don't know it yet." Lee Lee smiles. "Hi, Tyler," she says flirtatiously. Ty throws his head up.

The whole gang heads over, twins, Joz, and Telion. Ty gets up to offer any one of the girls a chair. Joz runs to it, says, "I will take it." I smile in my head. *He is such a gentleman.*

The twins and the boz sit on the grass. We all are eating, talking, looking up at stars. I turn back and see my parents enjoying themselves. They were over there, laughing talking about religion, politics, old war stories, to everyday life. The twins' mom bust out the dominos and cards; now it's really on. Spades, tunk, and bridge, they' bout to get it.

"It's going to be a long night. They 'bout to act up and do a lot of trash talking." I laugh.

"Hey," Joz says, "isn't that Mz. Cy'Queita our school counselor?"

"Gurl, you don't miss nothing." Lee Lee looks at Joz.

"Shouldn't," Joz replies with confidence.

We all look over and say in union, "Yelp, that's her."

The twins say, "She is our mom."

"Say what now. Why yawl never said nothing?" I look over at them.

"Because you never asked," Shareé says smartly.

"How was we supposed to ask something we didn't know?" Joz says with an attitude.

"You best watch your tone, heffa" Shareé snaps.

"Hey," Shará chimes in, "everyone, just chill. Now you know she's our mom."

"She is a good counselor," Mo' says.

"And how would we know that?" Joz asked.

"That's none of your business." Lee Lee jumps in.

"Because I have been to see her. She has helped me out a lot since that visit," Mo replied.

"Obviously." Joz looks.

"You really need to shut up like fo' real!" Shareé snaps.

"Why yawl getting on me?" Joz questions.

"Because you always in someone face or business when it doesn't concern you. Learn to stay in your lane," Shará says with sternness in her voice. Joz turns on her phone and mumbles something to herself. "Gurls," says the boz, look at each other and laugh.

I try to clear the air. "It's going to be a long night. I can bring the projector out, and we watch a movie."

"Naw, let's play a game like truth or dare, promise are repeat." Joz jumps up from her phone.

Lee Lee says, "I thought you was on your phone. That would be a game you would like to play nosy."

Joz rolls her eyes and say, "I will go first. Anyone?"

"Yeah, pick one," Shareé says with her lips curved up.

"Truth," Joz says.

"As if there is any in you." Shará laughs while she makes her eyes bigger and looks at Joz.

"Ask your question, Shareé." Joz give Shará no response.

"Why in the hell are you so nosy?" Shareé says as she eats a wang.

"Should have seen that one coming." Lee Lee looks at Joz.

"Because I'm a reporter," Joz replies.

"You are a freshman," Lee Lee says.

"I'm a reporter and will be one of the best when I grow up. I like reporting the facts. Getting all up in people's business, as yawl call it. It's fun."

"It's dangerous if you don't watch yourself," Shareé says with her fist balled up.

"Okay, next," Shará interrupts.

Lee Lee says, "I have a dare for you Tyler."

Ty looks over an says, "Which is?"

"You have to kiss me on the lips," Lee Lee says as she puts her finger up and pats her lip.

"*Ooooooooohhhh*," we all say.

"And what if I don't do the dare?" Ty ask as he thinks in his head. "I don't want my first kiss to be with Lee Lee. I have another gurl I would kiss with no dare."

"Then you will have to go up to the parents as they are playing spades and shout out a card in one of their hands."

"Well, I'm about to get killed 'cause I'm not kissing you." Ty begins to walk over to them.

We all look in suspense as Ty heads over to the spades table where my dad, Mo's granddad, Má, and Mz. Cy'Queita are playing. He looks into Mz. Cy'Queita hand and calls out the ace of spades while standing in between her and dad. Ty didn't see his mom watching the game; she popped him upside his head and told him to "go play." We all laughed so hard, falling all over each other. He ran back, saying, "Man, that's not funny."

"You should have kissed me then," Lee Lee says. Ty just looks at Lee Lee with aggravation.

Telion says, "Man, that was too funny. We thought you was going to be gone for real."

"Yeah, I know." Ty looks at Teli.

"You were scared, wasn't you?"

"Man…"

"Don't lie. You know you was."

"Yeah, I was. Now it's my turn," Ty says.

"Don't pick me because you mad." Lee looks at Ty.

"Yes, I can choose one." Ty points at Lee.

"*Dare!*" Lee shouts.

"I dare you to take Joz's phone and throw it in the fire." Ty points in Joz direction.

Before she could respond, Mo'Lynn snatched Joz's phone from her hands and threw it in the bomb fire, stood there, looked at Joz, and dusted her hands. Everyone got real quiet and just watched, looking in puzzlement and curiosity on what would happen next.

Joz got up out the wicker chair and charged at Mo'Lynn, and before we knew it, they were fighting. Going at them it tough too.

The boz tried to break it up, but it didn't work. My dad and Ty's dad came over and broke them up, each one holding a gurl.

My Má comes over, and by the look on her face, it's not going to be nice. "Now what is going on here? Carmella, speak now!"

"Aww, calm down, kids will be kids," Mo' grandmother says.

"Not like this and not in my home they want." My Má looks straight on at us all. "Carmella!"

"Má," I whine, "why do I have to say? I was watching like everyone else."

"Gurl," Má says with her arms crossed.

"We was playing a truth are dare, promise are repeat, and Ty dared Lee Lee to take Joz phone and throw it in the bomb fire, but the next thing we knew, Mo'Lynn took the phone and threw it in the fire 'cause that was the dare. Then they got to fighting."

Mz. Cy'Queita looked at the twins. "Gurls?"

They both said in unison, "Yes, ma'am, that's what went down."

"Why would yawl kids just watch?" Telion's dad chimes in.

"And why would you dare that, Tyler?" Ty's mom raised her hand to pop him again.

"Look, they are being kids. Can we get back to the spades now?" My father released Joz.

"Really, Big Daddy! Really!" Má says as she walks back up to the house.

"You gurls apologize to one another," Mz. Cy'Queita says.

They both look at each other. Mo'Lynns hair was twisted all over her head, and Joz got some braids missing. They both apologize. You know they don't mean it. As the parents began to walk away and get back to their game, Mo' whispered in Joz's left ear in an eerily scary voice, "Oh, this is nowhere near to being over."

As everyone is walking away, Joz shouts, "What about my phone?" No one replies.

We all sit back at the bomb fire. After spades, everyone starts to clean up. The boz grab all the trash and place them in our trash bins on the front curb. Us gurls starts to put the chairs away. The boz comeback to put up the card tables and chairs back in the shed. Mo'Lynn and her grandparents say good night. Mz. Cy'Queita and

Ty's mom are in the kitchen, helping my Má clean up the kitchen, as they sip on their wine. Telion, his father, Joz, and her parents head out. Teli's father says, "A healthy good night, ladies," while looking into Mz. Cy'Queita's eyes, walking out the front door. All three ladies say good night. Then in walk Tyler's dad and mine from the patio.

Ty's dad touches his mom on the waist and says, "Honey, you know there is church in the morning. Are you ladies done here?"

"Are we done, ladies?" Ty's mom asks as she sips the last of her wine and places the glasses in the dishwasher. "We are done. Yawl have a blessed night. We will see each other in service tomorrow," Má says.

"Teen Sunday school and teen church service," us youngster says in unison. We give out hugs as the rest head out.

As my father shuts the door, my Má right behind him, I head upstairs as I hear him say good night with a smile in his voice. Má kisses him dearly and says, "With many more to come, luv." To our rooms we go for the night. My parents close their door.

After I get all my things, I head to the shower my phone buzz. I look over at it and say to myself, "I will get it after I come from the shower." I wash the night off with hot water that I love. After my shower, I sit on the floor to journal a little bit. I get up, and then it dawns on me to check my phone. I grab it and lie down under the covers on my cotton plush pillow. I HAD A GREAT NIGHT. LOTS OF FUN KICKING IT WITH YA. SEE YOU IN CHURCH TOMORROW, Ty texts. I send back a smiling face, then hit the sack hard.

Sunday morning, O Sunday morning, you came a little too early. "Up and rise, sweetness! we don't want to be late." Má knocks at my door as she heads downstairs. We don't eat on Sunday mornings. It's called fasting. To me, it helps me hear that much clearer on what God is saying to me. I'm that much more submissive to the leading of the Holy Spirit. I'm ready to be used to help, give advice and just that warm smile of a hello. The anointing follows, which is much more powerful to me when I fast. We get in the car and head to service. Mz. Cy'Queita is our youth-school teacher. She is learning us on peer pressure. A teen-service elder follows suit with a motivational message from the books of Exodus and Romans. After service, everyone comes over for brunch.

We had bacon-wrapped pork in a blanket with and without cheese, waffles, pancakes, freshly squeezed orange juice, some cranberry juice, and eggs. The parents are on the patio eating and talking about the service and what events are coming up at church. We are chillin' on the grass, talking about what is to come of the week, like how we will be kicking major butt in sports and anything else we went out for. We talked about birthdays and what events will go on at church for us. We have an exciting teen ministry. Any and every time you come, you will get something out of it. Not too much later, the men clean, everyone head out, saying their "see ya lata's."

Sports, here we go. We all ran track and field together. Telion did baseball, basketball with Ty, twins basketball also, while me, Joz, and Lee Lee did volleyball. Mo'Lynn just came to support when it wasn't track season. Everyone also did cross-country; it helped prepare us for track. We had a real good track team. This morning practice wasn't no joke. After practice, we all hit the locker room. Months have went by since the fight between Joz and Mo'Lynn. They weren't buddy-buddy, but they were surface cool with each other. As we headed out the shower, with Joz always the last one out, we hear a loud scream come from her. She is screaming, jumping all around in the shower, going QRZ.

Coach Niles hurries in. "Joz, what is going on? What's the matter?" Joz kept jumping and screaming, jumping and screaming. "Calm down, I can't understand you!" Coach yells.

Joz screamed, "My hair! Something has dropped on my head!" Sure, as the day is long, it was something green in her head. All that jumping didn't help; what was in her braids was not coming out. It sat so still like it was stuck to her.

"Be very still," Coach says as she walks slowly up to her. She pulls out what looks like a poison dart frog from the top of her braids and says, "I wonder how that got in here? You will need to go see the nurse just to make sure everything is all right. Dry off, and I will walk you there after I let this frog out." Good thing Coach Niles was also our science teacher. As Joz comes into the locker room to dry off from her shower scare and head to the nurse, she looks so scared she keeps her head down in embarrassment, put her clothes on, and heads out with Coach to go to the nurse.

"Wow, that was QRZ," Shareé says.

"Yeah, I'm with ya," Shará replies.

"I wonder how that frog even got in there?" Lee Lee asked while laughing. "Well, I bet her butt want be the last one in the shower no more. Hahahahahaha!"

As we all are getting dressed, Mo'Lynn, with her eerie quietness, says nothing. We all began to leave and head for homeroom. *I told her this wasn't over. Huh, little do she know this is just the beginning,* Mo' says to herself.

We enter homeroom. Joz is still not back from the nurse. Shará fills the boz in on what happened to Joz in the gurl's locker room.

"No one pulls out their phones to record it?" Telion says.

"Joz is the one who always has her phone out, and besides, we were all shocked from the screaming and jumping around she was doing." Lee Lee chuckles as she is drawing something on her notebook.

"That's really not good. A number of things could happen to her if the frog really got on her skin. There could be swelling, nausea, and muscular paralysis," Tyler instructs us.

"So what you saying?" Shará asked.

Mo'Lynn interjects, "Since it was found in her head, it could swell. She could feel like she is going to throw up but don't. She could get migraines. She could even lose muscle function."

"Not cool. Not cool at all," Shareé says as she shakes her head.

"How do you know so much about what can happen, Mo'Lynn?" I look over to her with my arms folded.

"I was explaining in more detail to Shará's question." Mo' looks.

"Maybe, but you had this strange tone in your voice that you knew are wanted this to happen to her," I say in a questioning tone. Mo' doesn't agree or deny. Then the bell rings.

Meanwhile, Joz is at the nurse, and Mz. Au'bre is checking her over. "Honey, do you know how it got in your head?"

"You talking about the frog, right? What's going to happen to me? I'm not feeling too good."

"Just sit here. I'm going to give you a warm towel to wrap around your neck. So the nausea has set in. I'm going to call Mr. Fisher in just to be safe," Mz. Au'bre says, concerned.

"My father? Why would you do that?" Joz asked.

"Because you will be going home for the rest of the day," Mz. Au'bre states as she pats her shoulder. She slides her chair over to the phone, punches in the principal's extension. "Hello there, Mr. Fisher. I have Joz here in the nurse office. A situation happened in the girl's locker room this morning, and I'm going to have to send her home."

"Okay, I will be right over. Thank you." Mr. Fisher hangs up.

In comes Mr. Fisher. "Aww, young lady, what happened?" He bends down and touches Joz knee.

"I'm not feeling too good." Joz puts on a sad face.

"I have called your mother, and she will be up here to get ya. Okay?"

"Okay, Daddy." Joz tries to muster up a smile.

Not even thirty minutes later, Mrs. Fisher picks Joz up from the nurse and takes her home. "Go on up to your room and lie down. I will bring you up some soup, crackers, and that juice you like."

"Thanks, Mom," Joz says as she slowly makes her way upstairs to her room.

Mrs. Fisher goes in the kitchen and makes the soup, places it in a bowl with crackers on top and the juice all nicely placed on a serving tray. "Here, drink and eat. I will be up here later to check up on you." Mrs. Fisher sits the tray on the nightstand close to Joz. As she walks out, she looks back with her hand on the doorknob, says "My po' baby," and shuts the door. She goes downstairs, sits on the couch, grabs her laptop, and researches this poison frog.

We all meet up at lunch at the usual booth, and there is no Joz. "The nurse must have sent her home," I say.

"I wonder what her report will be on this?" Lee Lee chuckles.

"Chill out 'cause it's not cool on so many levels. Anybody done that to me, I would seriously kick their tail. I'm not playing. You don't play like that," Shareé says, angry and annoyed.

"Twin, since you are concerned, then if you want, we can go check on her after school." Shará looks a bit concerned herself.

"Naw, we can't. We have practice." Shareé bounces the basketball.

"Well, after that then." Shará snatch the ball away.

"Um, naw, let's just shoot her a text or call her. I don't want whatever she got to get on me."

"It's not contagious," I say. "Are is it?"

"No, it's not!" Ty says.

"Maybe we should go see her after school," I suggested.

"I can't. I have practice too." Teli shrugs his shoulders.

"I guess it's just Lee Lee, Mo'Lynn, Ty, and I that will go see Joz." I try to sound concerning enough to get a reaction out the others. After that, the bell rings for the last class of the day. Everything is still going as planned.

*Now I will know where Joz stay. Let the games commence.* Mo'Lynn smile to herself.

After school, we all get on Mo'Lynn's bus to head toward Joz's house. Mo' never paid attention that Joz was only a couple blocks from her house. Maybe 'cause most times Joz rode to school with her dad. Joz states she likes being the first at the school. She would listen in on the staff meeting so she would know what was going on. We get off the bus at Mo's stop and walk a couple blocks down to Joz's house.

"Did anyone think to bring or make a card?" Mo'Lynn ask.

"We all were at school with you, when was we supposed to do that?" I roll my eyes.

"And why?" Lee Lee asked. Ty just shook his head at us.

"I made her a card. I mean it's not much, just out of notebook paper I folded and wrote 'Get Well Soon' on the front," Mo' informs us. Then she asked, "Do you guys want to write something on the side?"

"That was a really nice thing of you," I said as I grabbed the folded paper card and wrote I HOPE YOU FEEL BETTA and signed. Everyone else signs by my name as we keep walking to Joz's house.

Ty knocks on the door, and Mrs. Fisher comes and open the door. As her mom opens the door, she welcome us in. We head into the living room. She lets us know that Joz is in the bed right now, but if we would like to see her, then we can go up for just a short time. We head up the stairs to Joz's room on the left. There she is in bed, not looking good. We give her the homemade card from Mo'Lynn that we all signed. I signed for Teli and the twins. She read what everyone wrote. Then we let her know that we just came by to see how she was doing and we would let her rest. She said thank you, and we headed down the stairs. We told Mrs. Fisher thanks for letting us stop by. Good thing we all didn't live too far from each other. We walked Mo'Lynn home first; she was a couple of blocks away. Ty and I stayed the farthest. We crossed the busy street and dropped Lee Lee off at her house, and then Ty dropped me at home.

"What a day, huh, Ty?"

He looks at me and say, "So are we going to find out who done this to Joz?"

"There is plenty of ways the frog could have gotten in her braids," I replied, looking at Ty.

"Nope. We don't have those frogs nowhere around here. Someone put that frog in her braids," Ty insists.

"Now who would do something like that." I make my eyes big at Ty.

He smiles and say, "That's what we have to find out." He hugs me then heads home.

Before I'm in the house good, my Má calls out to me. "Carmella, what in the world happen at school today? I got a call from Mrs. Fisher letting me know that you all went to her house after school to check on Joz. What really happened after practice?"

"Má, do we have to talk about it it's been a long day?" I whimper a bit.

"Yes, we do, young lady, because that is serious. What happened to her?" Má yells from the kitchen.

I go into kitchen, talking. "Joz was in the shower after cross-country practice. She is always the last one in the shower. The next thing we know, she is screaming and jumping all around, talking about something is in her braids. Coach Niles runs in to see what is going on. We all stand behind Coach as she grabs a towel and get the frog

27

out Joz's head. She takes the frog outside, then takes Joz to the nurse office." I began to sit on the stool

"So yawl didn't see who did it?" Má points the spoon in my face.

"Má,'" I say tiredly, "we was all in the locker room getting our clothes on. You asking what Ty asked. He says that we don't have poison frog around here."

"Well, he would know. That young man is smart as a whip. We do need to get someone to look into this," Má says with her lips in and upside-down grin. "When your father gets home, we will pray for Joz, her family, and for the person who did this to come clean."

"Do you really think they will, Má?" I lean my head on my hand.

"Prayer works, and if they know what's best for them."

Má starts to set the table. Dad gets home, and Má fills him in over dinner. What a dinner and deep discussion. We had homemade pasta with ground turkey meat over it with mozzarella and Mexican four cheese smoothed all over it, corn on the cob, hot water cornbread, tea, and broccoli.

"That's a shame what happen to Joz today." Dad shakes his head.

"Bae, do you think it has something to do with the fight the girls had a couple weeks back." I hear Má stating.

"Naw, it wasn't that serious," Dad says sarcastically.

"It can't be no coincidence, honey. Someone put a frog in that child's head." Má sounds really concerned.

"Don't go get your bra all out of whack. We don't know neither how it got there." Dad takes a sip of his tea.

"Well, don't you think someone needs to find out because this could really be fatal to her." Má chews her meat.

"We can cover all of them in prayer," Dad says as he takes a fork full of broccoli. I think to myself, *My Má and dad are always on one accord.* "If it makes you feel any betta, we can throw in there, 'If it was a person, then they will come clean about it.'" Dad rubs Má on the shoulders.

Má is calm now, and you can see and tell she has already been praying. She doesn't play when it comes to prayer! It's like my Má has her lips pressed up to God's ears, like they are best buds or something. "The ladies and I will be praying about this at prayer circle tomorrow," Má speaks sternly. You can see the expression on my dad's face like *Really*, but he doesn't say anything. He knows how Má can get when prayer comes up. He just smiles.

We all finish dinner. I clean the kitchen. Dad takes the trash out, and Mom is on the porch on the phone with Mz. Cy'Queita, Ty's Mom, and Lee Lee's mom. All I hear is, "Hold on. We have to call Ms. Fisher."

I head upstairs to my room and call Joz. "Hey gurl, the mothers are all on the phone talking about what happen today after practice. How are you doing?"

"I'm still very nauseated. My mom says she is taking me to the doctor tomorrow *early*. She researched the symptoms, and I already have one, so she is going to make sure 'cause that means the others want be too far behind."

"Can you remember what happen? Like when you felt the frog in your braids?"

"To be honest, no. I remember showering then about to let the water run threw my braids, and as my hands went up to separate them a bit, I felt something."

I sat up on my pillow to the headboard. "Do you think someone did this to you?"

"Who would do something like that?"

"That's what I said, but Má and Ty are so sure someone did."

"I don't know, I'm just ready for it all to be over."

"So you taking your braids out, do you need help?"

"Naw, Mom and I will have them out by end day tomorrow. We are starting right after my doc appointment. I will miss school Tuesday because if I feel betta, Mom made me an appointment to get them redone."

"Your mom not playing, she keeps your hair braided. I remember that since middle school."

"My mom don't know how to comb hair. She takes me to my aunt's shop."

"Hey, have you told your aunt yet?"

"Mom says she will tell her once we get to the shop. You know how my aunt is. She is straight-up thug. Ain't no telling what she is going to say."

"Well, let me know cause your aunt is funny. I will get all your work for ya and bring it by so you will at least be caught up and want fall behind."

"Thanks, Carmella, you are a true friend."

"Np. Now get some rest. I will check in tomorrow."

I head downstairs and see Dad on the couch, watching another one of those action-suspense TV shows. I head out the front door. Má is still on the big swing, chatting it up with the ladies. I sit on the porch steps with my journal, taking in the breeze. I couldn't let today pass without writing in my journal. So much action, mystery, and folks wired up like my Má and Shareé. I smile as I finish my entry for Monday. What a day—Monday.

# CHAPTER 3

OFF TO THE DOCTOR'S office Mrs. Fisher and Joz head. Má says it was 7:00 a.m. when they left. Once I was downstairs, about to head to the bus, Má and the other ladies was on the prayer line going in for them. I say "Amen" as I head out the door. I meet Ty at the bus stop. I must have been running a little late 'cause as I get there, the bus was pulling up. As we get on the bus, Ty says, "So running a little late, are we?" I give him a frowned-up look. He smiles as we take our seats. We pick up Lee Lee at her stop, then off to school.

"It feels a little weird that Joz is not in homeroom." Lee Lee says, picking at her pen top.

"Oh really, as much as you two get into it?" I say.

"I know right," Lee Lee say with half a smile.

Teli comes over with his baseball mitt in hand. "Hey there."

"Hello." I smile.

"So how is Joz doing? My apologies I couldn't come with you guys yesterday I had practice. You know how it is right?" he asked.

"Naw, bro, we don't," Ty says, a little snappy.

"Yeah, it's cool. You can let her know when you see her. Mo'Lynn made up a card, so I signed it for you and the twins," I said.

"Thanks a lot," Teli says.

"So have you heard anything else from Joz, Carmella?" Mo'Lynn asked.

"And why do you want to know, miss thang? Yawl don't get along. But it was cool that you came with us yesterday and the card." Lee Lee looks Mo'Lynn up and down.

"I'm a little concerned." Mo' looks at Lee Lee with sad eyes, as she says to herself, *I have to play this off real cool. They want ever find out it was me. They can't find out. Then all the others will come out too.*

Ty says, "I think someone did this to her and we have to find out who."

"You have been saying that since yesterday. Then my Má said it at dinner." I sit straight up in my desk.

"You know what though, Carmella, Tyler is right. What will we do when we find out who it is?" Teli ask.

"Let's just find out first, then we can get to that." Lee Lee snaps. No one is paying attention, but after Ty said what he said, Mo's eyes got big, and she got weird quiet.

"Mo'Lynn, what you think?" Teli says. Before she could answer the bell rings.

First, second, third, and fourth period, yes, it was now lunch. The whole gang will be there, and we can see what's we got to do to find who did this to Joz. Shará pulls her phone out and start to text Joz. Shareé grabs her hand. "Um, what you think you are doing? We are not supposed to have our phones out at school. You know what Mom said!"

"Girl, chill out. She want know unless you tell. It's just a little text." Shará snatches her arm back and texts, HEY JOZ, JUST CHECKING ON YA. MAKING SURE YOU ARE OK, adding a peace sign. "See there, now I'm going to put my phone away. You are such a goody-goody."

"Don't start on me, shut." Shareé says aggressively.

By this time, we are all on the patio at our usual spot. "Sooo what are we going to do?" Ty asked.

"Do about what?" Shareé sips her juice.

"Oh, yawl don't have homeroom with us."

"Right, 'cause we have b-ball practice," Shará says.

"You just really on one today." Lee Lee rolls her eyes.

"As I was saying," Ty interjects. "We was discussing what we are going to do when we find out who did this to Joz."

"How are we supposed to know who did it? 'Cause you know I'm always ready to bust a head." Shareé jumps up and down with her fist up, like she is in the ring.

Under her breath, Mo' sneakily says, *Yawl will never find out.*

"Mo'Lynn, did you say something?" I look over at her.

"Um, nope, I was just thinking out loud, I guess." She looks over at me.

"What were you thinking?" Lee Lee looks at her with suspicion.

"Just that…um nothing really." Mo' looks a little scared.

"*Uh-huh!*" Shareé responds like she is ready to bust Mo' right now. She leans over and whisper in Sharà ear, "We going to have to keep an eye on this chick because she is too weird for me!"

"Since there are no poisonous frogs around these parts, a person must have brought it in the locker room," TY implies. We all looked puzzled. Then he asks a question, "So where was everyone actually when Joz, well, yawl heard her screaming?"

"We were all in the locker room getting dressed," I answer.

"So everyone was together around each other?" Ty asked with his eyebrow up.

"Well, the twins were at their lockers, Lee Lee and I sitting on the bench talking." I pointed to each person to say where I think they were. Before I got to Mo'Lynn, the cafeteria monitor came.

"Excuse me, what are you kids still doing out here?"

We all look at her questioningly.

"The bell rang ten minutes ago."

"What!" I scream.

"Dang, now we late for class!" Shareé say as she gets her ball and backpack.

We were so deep on what was going on we lost track of time. Everyone started to head their separate ways, and Lee Lee said, "Hey, where did Mo'Lynn go? She bet not had left when the bell rang and didn't say nothing."

"I don't think she would do that." I look at Lee Lee.

We get to fifth period. "What the what?" Lee Lee looks over at Mo'. "She right here in class. Why you didn't say nothing, Mo'Lynn?" Lee Lee sounds very annoyed.

"I didn't hear the bell myself. I saw people heading out, so I left too," Mo' says, a little squeamish.

"You could have warned us. That's really not cool," I said as I sat down.

"Yawl just a little tarty. Nothing going to happen," Mo' sarcastically gestured.

"It betta not!" Lee Lee slams her books on her desk.

Mr. Fitz had begun to learn us on US history until he heard us talking. "Ladies, this is a warning. Don't be late again."

"Yes, Sir," we say as we look over at Mo'Lynn with evil eyes. Mo' looks back with an evil smirk of her own.

Mr. Fitz gives us our homework for the day, and we head out of class. Sixth, seventh periods, then back on the long yellow bus we go. I barely get to sit down when Ty speaks up. "You can finish what you were saying at lunch." Ty looks at me over the seat as I sit down.

"Can I get good in my seat first, Ty?" Lee Lee sat with attitude.

"Okay, yawl are seated. Finish." Ty rolls his hands as to say like "Come on with it."

"I was about to point at Mo' before the cafeteria monitor stopped me. You know what, I don't remember seeing her when we were getting dressed. Do you, Lee?" I look over at her.

"I barely pay Mo'Lynn any attention." She looks at her nails.

"Stop lying because you was saying something about her when we was leaving late after lunch," I said with my lips pushed out with head tilted in disbelief.

"All I said was she left us and didn't even say nothing. She knew the bell had rung." Lee Lee looks at me. I can see her aggravation.

Ty looks at us. "Yeah, that was messed up."

The bus starts to move, and he sits down. "A little, huh," snaps Lee Lee with her arms folded. "I don't remember seeing her. Do you think?"

"Naw, she ain't that QRZ." I look so unassured.

"We really don't know if she is or isn't because we don't know her like that." We can hear Ty in the seat behind us.

We just sat there with our thoughts, didn't realize how quite we got until the bus pulled up at Lee Lee's stop. "See yawl lata," Lee says as she grabs her backpack and heads off the bus. Our stop has come up shortly after Lee Lee's.

Ty walks me to my door still with a puzzled look of unbelief and curiosity on his face. "Lata, Carmella."

"See ya." I wave my hands and go in the house.

The school week is over. I sent a mass text to everyone to see if we all could hang out and figure more out what happened to Joz. I'm waiting on everyone to reply. Speaking of which, Joz never got back to me about her doc appointment 'cause she haven't been to school for the rest of the week. I'm about to call her up.

*Ring, ring.* "Hey, gurl! Wuz up?" Joz sounds a lot betta.

"Did you forget something?" I ask smartly.

"Ummmmmmm…nope." It sounds like she is eating something.

"Are you sure?" I grab the phone a little tighter. "You sound a lot betta you was—"

"Oh yeah, my apologies. I was supposed to call you back to tell you about my doc appointment, all that good stuff. As you know, we went Tuesday morning. They ran a bunch of test, took my blood, and the test just came back this morning. I just had the symptoms of the nausea. As far as my brain and everything, I'm good. No swelling are nothing." Joz sounds relieved.

"We were all concerned."

"Aww, yawl missed me."

"Don't get off the subject." I had to bring her back to the convo.

"So after my doc appointment, we went to my aunt's shop. She is not having it. Her and my mom going back and forth 'cause my aunt wants to get the person that done this and my mom remind her that God says vengeance is his."

"Wait a minute, so your aunt think it is someone too!" My voice gets a little higher.

"Yelp, she said there is no way that one frog will just appear out of nowhere. As long as she been living here, which is a long time, I might add. She hasn't heard are seen anything about poisonous frog!"

"I told you your aunt would know. She gets around."

"Yeah, she does." We both laugh. "My aunt told my mom when she finds out who did it that she needs to sue them. You know how my mom is. She said to let her pray on it."

"Hey, I was wondering if you could get out? I'm trying to get everyone together so we can see who, what, and how the frog got in your braids. Má, Ty, and now your aunt is saying that someone did this. So now we all need to find out who. I sent a mass text out to everyone. I'm waiting for them to reply back." I lay back on the throw pillows.

"How about we go to the new burger place, then walk over to the skate park? I have been cooped up in this house I'm ready to break out." Joz is getting ready as we speak.

"Let's say about 1:00 p.m. 'cause you know Teli and the Twins have b-ball practice every Saturday morning," I say sarcastically.

"Kool. I will see yawl there. Don't tell them I'm coming. Yawl know yawl missed me, and I want it to be a surprise." You can hear her rambling, throwing her stuff.

"Surprise it will be," I said, laughing as I hang up.

After the phone, text messages started coming through.

Twins: YEAH WHAT TIME? YOU KNOW WE HAVE PRACTICE?

Ty: YOU KNOW I'M THERE. WE CAN RIDE TOGETHER. MY DAD WILL DROP US OFF. WAIT, WHERE ARE WE GOING?

Teli: I'M DOWN. CAN IT BE AFTER LUNCH TIME.

Lee Lee: ARE YOU STILL COMING FOR YOUR MANI PEDI TOMORROW? WE CAN LEAVE TOGETHER?

Me: WE WILL MEET AT THE NEW BURGER PLACE AT 1 THEN WALK OVER TO THE SKATE PARK. YES I'M STILL COMING TOMORROW.

I sent Ty a separate text after the mass one.

Me: HEY I HAVE A MANI PEDI IN THE MORNING SO IF YOU AND YOUR DAD WANT TO PICK ME UP FROM THE SHOP AND LEE LEE THEN YES WE CAN ALL RIDE TOGETHER.

Ty: I FIGURED THAT AFTER READING THE MASS TEXT.

—I WANTED TO MAKE SURE IT WAS KOOL THAT'S WHY I SENT YOU A PERSONAL ONE. <<Insert surprised-face emoji>>

—YOU KNOW I WILL HAVE DAD SCOOP YOU UP SO WE CAN HEAD OUT. OH YEAH LEE LEE TOO, he sends back.

—DON'T BE LIKE THAT TY.

—WHAT? SHE LIKES ME LIKE THAT AND I DON'T LIKE HER THAT WAY. LEE LEE IS KOOL AND ALL, SHE AIN'T FOR ME.

—WELL YOU NEED TO TELL HER THAT.

—YOU KNOW I WILL. I WILL SEE YOU TOMORROW CARMELLA.

After all the texting, I head downstairs just in time for dinner. Yes, time to eat, and I can let my parents know what us teens (I love the sound of that) will be doing Saturday. As I sat the table for dinner, we were treated to a great spread. We have baked pork chops, mashed potatoes with brown gravy, sting green beans, and fresh brewed tea. This time, Má has put all kinds of fruit in there.

"Hey, dear parents of mine." I set the last cup on the table.

They both look at each other and smile in unison. "Yes, dear."

"Is it okay if I go to the new burger place and then afterwards the skate park with the crew, and, Má, can you drop me off so Lee Lee can do my mani-pedi tomorrow morning? Ty's dad will take myself, Lee Lee, and Ty to the burger joint," I said as I sat down.

"You have it all figured out, so I'm good with it. What about you, bae?" Má looks over at me.

"Me too," Dad agreed.

After dinner, I cleaned up and headed upstairs, looked at my phone, and saw Lee Lee had sent some designs for my mani-pedi. They are all cute. I replied back, I WILL LET YOU DECIDE with a smiley.

Saturday morning comes. I smell the cool but smooth breeze of autumn. "Thank you, Lord, for another day," I prayed as I head out of bed and look out the window. It feels so right today. So right. I get dressed. I can smell Má's cooking, already placing food on the table.

"Good morning, honey bunch," she says as she kisses me on the forehead.

"Morning, Má," I said as I began to sit at the table. Dad brought out three cups and the pitcher of orange juice. He placed them all on the table, pitcher in the middle cups in their places. "Morning, Dad," I muster up.

"Morning, honey," Dad says as he takes his seat at the head of the table. I'm in the middle, and Má is across from me, right next to Dad. Dad says grace, and we chaw down on eggs over easy, bacon sausage, and homemade rolls.

"So what does your day look like, Dad?" I asked as I put a roll in my mouth.

"I'm going to mow the yard front and back, play around in the garage with my old car, then after that, who knows." He sips his orange juice.

"What about you, Má?" I look over at her as she is about to place some eggs in her spoon.

"I'm going to drop you off after we clean the kitchen. I will go to Mrs. Fisher's. We are having prayer cycle over there and brunch. We will also have book-club meeting as well. I should be home about three maybe. You can call me once you are done at the skateboard park if you need a ride back home."

"I will. Thanks, Má."

I start to collect the dishes so we can clean up. After breakfast, we all head out. Mom kisses Dad and says, "If you need are want anything while I'm out, let me know."

Dad hugs Má tight and says, "All I need and want is you."

Má smiles like a kid in the candy store. As they embrace, I watch and say to myself, *One day, one day.*

After I hug Dad, Má and I get in the car. I yell out the window as Má is pulling out the driveway, "See you lata, Dad!"

"Love you too, sweetheart! Yawl enjoy," he says as he brings the mower out.

We both holler as Má is starting down in the street, "Love you too!"

I'm so excited to head to the Shopen to get my nails and feet done—a gurl has to keep herself up and to chill with er body today. As Má pulls into the parking space, I wave bye as I get out the car. As you open the door to the Shop, the bells hanging from the glass door makes a sound to announce that someone is coming in. The young lady behind the bar-shaped counter was just about to say, "Can I help you? I assume—" But Lee Lee looks at her before she gets a word in and says, "She's with me."

Lee takes me over to the spa chair for my pedicure. For her to only be fourteen, going to be fifteen in January, she knows her stuff. She has other clients too, but you already know I come first. LOL. She works part time in her mother's Shopen. She tell me all the time it doesn't feel like work, as she is having a great time. She loves what she does, and it shows. Lee is always learning and trying to do her best. Those camps, her practicing is really paying off.

"Let me know if the water is too hot," Lee says. As she gets everything prepared, she is talking as everyone else in here, holding their own little convos.

"So what all are we doing today, Carmella?"

"After we are done here, Ty father is going to come get us and take us to the new burger place, then we are walking over to the skate park." As I'm going on and on, Lee Lee has started daydreaming about what, who knows. So I'm talking about this and that. I can see your mouth moving, but I don't hear a word coming out. Her thoughts has run to her and Ty being together.

"Lee, Lee what you thinking 'cause you was gone?" I wiggle my foot in front of her.

"Oh, my apologies, I was daydreaming about me and Tyler."

"You and Ty?" I ask questioned her.

"Yes, Tyler and I. You never know, Carmella, you never know."

I look at her with a smile. *Shud I tell her what Ty said? I don't think I shud*, I'm thinking to myself. Yes, even though they are both my friends, Ty told me that in confidence. So that means I won't be telling her.

She has placed this pretty pink glow-in-the-dark color on my big toes with these gold zigzag stripe design. "Is the gold glow-in-the-dark too?" I ask.

"Nope, but that would be cool, huh." Lee begins to put the gel machine on my feet. "I will have to bring that up to my mom and see what she can come up with. Come over here to the table so I can do your manicure." She helps me over to the table to sit.

Mrs. Leng walks by. "Your toes are looking really good, Carmella. You are getting so much better all the time, Lee." She pats me on my shoulder.

Lee does my manicure the same as my toes, but my thumbnails have her own creative touch. I hold my hands up and say, "Yelp, always on point."

Lee Lee smiles, then we all hear the bells on the door. Someone is coming in. We look, and there is Ty, right on time. "You ladies ready?" he asks as he leans on the counter.

"Yelp, we just finished. You came in right on time," Lee Lee says as I slip her forty dollars, including her tip.

As we head out, Lee Lee says bye to her mom. She says it back. We all smile and head out the glass door with the bells hanging. Into the car, we are almost in when Mrs. Leng comes out, "Remember, Lee, your dad will be picking you up after he is done at the cigar shop."

"Okay, Mom," Lee Lee says as she gets in the car.

"You guys ready to do whatever yawl plans are today?" Ty's dad says.

"Yelp," Ty says. "We want be doing much, but the much we will do will be fun."

His dad smiles looks at us through the rear view mirror in the car. We just shook our heads.

We made it to the new burger joint. "Thanks," we all say, shut the door, and head in. There is a HELP WANTED sign in the window. I look at Lee Lee and say, "I'm applying to work here for sure."

"You should, you should." Lee Lee was shaking her head up and down.

"Do you have time to work, Carmella?" Ty looks over at me.

"Yeah, I do part time. I can save up my long green and get me a car, then its 'Bye-bye, big yellow bus.'" I smile.

"You can't drive till your sixteen," Ty replies.

"Welp, that gives me a year after my birth in Oct. Plenty of time to save up and pay for driver's ed. Oh yes."

"When you get your G-ride, don't forget about us," Lee Lee says as she pushes my shoulder.

We three look up, and already waiting at the booth are the twins and Teli. I think to myself, *Someone is missing.* Joz is showing up a little bit later 'cause she wants to surprise everyone. So who else is not here? I'm thinking hard as we walk over to the booth, still having a brain fart as everyone is greeting each other.

"So yawl hungry?" Teli says, looking over at the menu.

Shareé shouts, "Shut yeah, we coming from practice, and my stomach is touching my spin."

"You not that hungry. Stop exaggerating." Shará pushes Shareé.

"How you going to tell me?" Shareé pushed her back.

"'Cause we twins, I'm hungry too, but my back not touching my spin." Shará got her lips poked out.

"Well, you not *me*!" Shareé rolled her eyes.

We all just look at them. I'm just shaking my head. Teli says, "Twins" and laughs. "Okay I will get everyone's order and then bring them back." Teli started to walk to the line to order.

"Kool." Shareé sucks her teeth.

"I'm coming with you, Teli. I want to get an application."

"To do what?" Shará questions me.

"To work here, of course," I say as I'm walking to get in line.

"You always doing something." Shará gestures with her hand.

"That's the way it works," I shot back as I make my way right next to Teli in the line.

Teli is placing everyone's order, and I see the manager. "Hello, my name is Carmella, and I would like an application. I seen the HELP WANTED sign in the window." I reached out my hand for him to shake. My parents helped me out with first impressions and interviewing when I told them I was ready to start working. My grades have to stay up, chores still have to be done, and stay in the sports I have started.

He reaches back and shakes my hand and says, "Sure. After you fill out the application, I can interview you if you have time."

"Yes, sir," I say as I take the application.

I headed over to an empty table, pulled out a pen from my backpack purse, and began to fill it out. I get to the days and hours I'm able to work. *Welp*, I think to myself. When I'm at school, all-week practice for cross-country is in the morning before school, right along with track practice, which also happens after school when it's that season. Don't know the day of volleyball yet, but it's after school. I have youth group on Wednesday, and I'm not working on Sunday. *The Lord rested, and so will I*, I say to myself with a smile on my face. So that leaves Monday, Tuesday, Thursday, and Saturday. Saturday after meets and games, even before maybe. Not bad for days a week, oh yeah. I just hope I'm not too tired 'cause I got to save up for me a G-ride.

I take the application to the manager. We went back to the booth I was just at. He looks over my application, sees my availability, asks me some questions. Then he looks at me and says, "How about you start Monday? Since you are only fifteen, I can't work you more than four hours a day. So from five to nine right now, Monday, Tuesday, and Thursday. Saturday, if you have turned in your work permit, I can place you on the schedule for four to ten. I will try to give you as many hours as you need, but in keeping this job, you must keep a GPA of at least a 3.0. We have high standards here. Do you think you can do that?" He looks me straight in the eye.

"Yes, sir," I said as I reached out to shake his hand. I'm always presentable. You never know when your opportunity will come. I have on my basic leggings with open-toe sandals 'cause I just got my feet done, tunic shirt, and my jean jacket that matches my leggings.

As the manger leaves, I text my parents and let them know that I have a *job* and my work schedule. I will need to get a work permit. I will finish telling them all the details once I get home. I get up to go where the crew is, and Joz walks in.

"Hey, er'body, yawl miss me?" Joz raises up her hands

Everyone says, "Yeahhhh!" gets up and give her hugs.

"I didn't know you was coming. It's good to see ya. Are you hungry?" Teli asked.

"Sure"

"What do you want, and I will get it for ya." He sips his drink.

Teli goes to get Joz's order. Everyone is excited to see her. We all sit down at the booth, laughing, just happy we all back together.

"So how long can you be out?" Shará puts fries in her mouth.

"Oh until whenever. I have been stuck in the house I'm so happy to be out." Joz does a sigh of relief.

"Thanks, Telion, I'm about to tear this up," Joz says as she takes a bite of the burger.

"No problem." Teli smiles.

"Okay, let's get back focused," Ty demands. "We need to figure out who and why someone would do this to Joz. Any takers?"

"I really just don't know." Lee Lee looks at Ty.

"Can yawl remember anything from that day? Where was yawl? Who was all there? Who wasn't there?"

"My man is so smart." Lee touches Ty's arm.

"I'm not your man." Ty moves his shoulder to get her hand off him. "Since we got everyone that was here that day, right?" Ty looks over, and Shará says, "Yeah."

"Hold up! Ummm, someone is missing. Where is Mo'Lynn?" Shareé eyes starts looking around.

I start to look a little guilty. "I don't have her number, so I didn't invite her. I didn't realize it till just now." I'm looking at my phone.

"Was she with yawl in the locker room the whole time even after Joz screamed?" Ty looks at us all sternly.

"Come to think about it. No." Lee Lee is patting her lips with her finger.

"We can't accuse her until we know for sure," Teli says.

"You right, bro." Ty looks though he already has.

"So that means we need to ask her, but not to be, ummm, what's the word I'm looking for?" I look up to see if anyone can give me a word.

I hear Shareé's voice. "'Pushy,' 'mean,' 'judging.' Like we already know she did it, we just want her to say it. Is that enough words?"

"I guess so." I look at her, shaking my head.

"So who going to ask her?" Shareé looks over at me.

"I will," Shará says. "She kinds of like me, and I want bully her like some." She looks over at her twin.

"When will you ask her and how?" Lee Lee looks up at Shará with one eyebrow raised.

"I think you should befriend her a little more, we all should. So that way, you might not have to ask her nothing. She might just come out and say it," Joz says. "I have been doing some research on her 'cause I told yawl she is a weird quiet, and stuff just get weirder and weirder. Let her open up too us."

"So this want get solved anytime soon, but ya best know I will keep it to the forefront 'cause I want answers!" Ty hits the booth table.

"We all do, man. Chill out a bit." Teli looks over at Ty.

"So we going to play her?" Lee Lee looks at the boz.

"No, I say we not going to be fake, but she did are did not say she was in the locker room. She shoul was at practice that morning, that much I do know. I don't remember seeing her when Joz screamed, though neither after the fact." I look at Joz.

"You wouldn't have. Neither of us would because we was concerned about what was going on." Shareé looked concerned for once.

"We will get the answers. Are we done here?" Shará starts to put her stuff in the trash and heads out the door. We clean our stuff up too and head behind Shará.

We cross the street to go to the skate park. Lee Lee looks over and says, "Hey, did you get the job?"

I look over. "You know I did, gurl." We both do a little dance. "I start Monday. I'm so excited. I have to get a work permit."

Lee looks and says, "If you don't know where to go, then I can show you. I already have mine. Once we are sixteen, then we want need it anymore."

"I know that too." We both sat on the bench.

While at the skate park, the boz and Shareé go hard on the boards. Myself and Joz can skate but decide to take it easy. Lee Lee and Shará just watch, chill, and talk on the swings at the park right next to them.

"What are you doing on that phone?" Lee reaches for Joz's phone.

Joz snatched it back. "I'm doing research, seeing if Mo'Lynn has any social media, anything I can find on her."

We all look at each other and say, "She's back!" singing in unison as we all laugh.

"You overjoyed about getting your phone back, huh, Joz?" Lee Lee asked.

"You darn right. My parents wasn't going to get me another one, but after what happen, my mom insisted." She cheesie with excitement.

"So you can say this is a blessing from a curse." I lean in to see what she will say.

"Well, the curse is over, and the blessings are just now starting." Joz laughed but did not look up from her phone.

So after about some hours at the skate park, it's getting dark. We wasn't even paying attention; we was having so much fun. We didn't notice the time until Teli's dad, Mr. John, pulled up. Then shortly came Mz. Cy'Queita for the twins, then Sr. for Ty, me, and Lee Lee.

"Can you drop me off at the cigar shop, Daddy Sr.?" Lee Lee says as she gets in the car.

"Sure." Sr. smiles.

We all know that Lee Lee is feeling Ty, but he is not having it. "He's not your dad, Lee Lee," Ty says, annoyed.

"I know, not right now at this moment, Tyler, but he will be." Lee Lee tries to look over the seat.

Ty doesn't say anything. I'm in the back with Lee, just looking curiously to what is going to happen. We get to the cigar shop, and Mr. Keanu is locking the door, heading toward us. "Right on time, brother" Mr. Keanu says to Sr.

Lee gets out the car. "See yawl lata." She looks right at Ty.

"Leave him alone, Lee Lee. Go get in the car." Mr. Keanu laughs and shuts the door.

We headed out the parking lot and shortly after pulled up to my home. "Hey, Dad, I will just walk home. I'm going to make sure Carmella well get in okay," Ty said.

"I have taught you will." Sr. smiles. As Sr. drives out the driveway up the street, we are waving 'til we don't see him anymore.

We sat on the porch. Ty says, "You have a good time today?"

"Yeah, I really did. What about you?" I look up at the stars.

"I always have a good time when I'm around you."

Ty is flirting. I look over at him. "Are you flirting with me?"

"What do you think?" Ty grabs my hand. I sit and look at him.

Má comes to the screen door. "Hello, Tyler, how are things with ya?" She holds two glasses of homemade lemonade.

"It's all good, Mrs. Carmel. Thanks for the drink." Ty lets my hand go to get the cup.

"Just a little bit longer, Carmella, then it's time to come in." Má walks back into the house.

"Okay, Má." I take my cup.

"Your mom is the best, and the lemonade is on point." Ty takes a big gulp.

"She is, isn't she?" I take a sip of mine.

Ty hands me the cup and say, "I will see you at youth group tomorrow." I get up to head into the house and hear Ty say, "I want to see you in more places than that."

I turn back. "Did you say something?"

"Naw, I will see ya," he says as he backs off and starts to head home.

I take the cups to the kitchen, rinse them out in the sink. I say good night. My phone has text message. I see the one I sent to my parents.

"Má, Dad," I say as I head down the stairs, "I wanted to tell you guys about my job."

"Oh yeah, sweetheart, tell us all about it." Má clicks off the TV.

"I interviewed right there. I have my work schedule already. I have to keeps my grades up, nothing less than a B-, and I have to get a work permit."

"Oh, I'm liking this already," my dad says.

"Well, look at God, my." Má raises her hands.

We all smile. I hug them, then as I'm about to go back upstairs, Dad asks, "Do you know where you are going for this permit?" Dad looks over the couch.

"Lee says she will let me know how and where to go. I think yawl will have to sign something." I start heading upstairs.

"Once you get all the info, let me know and I will take you," Má says.

"Thanks, Má!" I yell from the top of the stairs heading to my room.

I began to look at my text messages. Ty sends me one, of course. IT WAS FUN WITH YA TODAY. I HOPE WE CAN DO IT AGAIN WITHOUT EVERYONE. I smile, and before I know it, I text back OK and hit send, then realize too late. *Oh my, what have I done? What will Ty and I? Is this…will it be a date? Will Lee and I still be friends? Oh my, what have I done!* I say frantically.

# CHAPTER 4

SUNDAY MORNING, CHURCH TIME. I love teen youth church. It gives perspective on Scripture. It helps with life.

As we enter church, everyone is greeting each other. I smile, let my parents know that I'm heading to youth church. As I get to the room, Ty waves and says, "Hey." "Hello," I said as I sat next to him. We all are waiting for Mz. Cy'Queita to come in so we can discuss our lesson. Everyone begins to take their seats.

"Well hello, everyone. How are you guys this morning?" Mz. Cy'Queita stands in front of the group.

"Good," everyone say in unison.

"Today we will discuss friendship. What it means, how to go about building one things of that nature."

*Is she serious right now?* I'm thinking to myself with my brows frowned.

"How do you think a friendship even comes about?"

"It comes from liking that person," one of the teens says.

"Yes, that's a start. Anyone else?" Mz. Cy'Queita ask.

"Having some of the same things in common," another teen speaks up.

"Yes, good ones. Open your Bible to Proverbs 27:9, and we will also look at Matthew 22:39."

As Mz. Cy'Queita is talking, all I can think about is how or if I should tell Lee Lee. Or should I go hang with Ty and if it's nothing it's nothing, but if it turns into something, then I will let her know? Do I even want it to turn into something? Yes, Ty, is very handsome, very smart, and I like him. But as a friend or something more?

Uhhhhhh, this is all just too much to think about. Before I knew it, I blasted out a question. "What if you are in a situation to where someone likes a person the person don't like them, but they like another person, and they are all friends. What should you do?"

"Wow, that's a lot," Mz. Cy'Queita says. "I think the best thing to do is to know if these people even like each other more than friends. Then if you do, then for the respect of one another, you can let the other person know that. Yes, they might be hurt, but they know that you care and respect them enough to come and let them know. That's being a good friend. Think of how you would feel if you was that person. Would you want to be told?"

"Thanks so much, Teach." I smile.

"You are so welcome, Carmella." Mz. Cy'Queita looks down at the Bible to get us to read a verse.

Now you see why I love coming to youth Sunday school and youth group on Wednesday because I always get clarity on what I need. We go for a short break then come back in for teen church. The youth pastor speaks right in line with what youth class was about.

On the ride home, I began to think how do I even tell Lee Lee. Thinking about it, I do like Ty more than a friend. But I also like Teli. But I really don't see us together as a couple. To be honest, I think I'm attracted to him cause he is a bad boy, kind of. To me, there is nothing wrong with that because he is also cool, handsome, and a gentleman at times. Sweet like. Oh journal, what must I do? Who must I choose? Wait, Teli has never even asked me out. We just flirt with each other all the time. Hopefully, it's just a friendly date with Ty, and then I will know everything for sure. I have made up my mind. I, for sure, am telling Lee Lee after I see how the date goes with Ty. Naw, I'm just going to tell her.

"Hey, Carmella, you a awfully quiet back there. What's on your mind?" Má looks at me through the rearview mirror.

"Ty asked me out on a date next Friday." I start to say.

"That's nice." Má smiles.

"Yeah, but Lee Lee has a huge crush on him." I shrug my shoulders, unsure of what to do.

"Oh my." Má shakes her head.

"Ty has already let her know that he doesn't like her." I look down at my journal.

"Then that settles it, honey. Ty has made it known, but I can hear in your voice there is some concern." Dad doesn't look away from the road.

"Of course, Dad. Lee Lee is my friend, and I'm going to tell her about the date that Ty and I will go on." I look up at the back of the driver seat.

"So why are you concerned if you are going to tell her?" I hear the blinker Dad pushed.

Má hits Dad on the shoulder. "You are such a man."

Dad looks over at Má and says, "Thank you," with laughter in his voice.

"Carmella feels concerned because they are friends. She don't want to hurt Lee Lee because Ty likes her and not Lee Lee." Má looks back forward.

"Ohhhhhhhh!" Dad is catching on now. "Just be truthful with her no matter what," he assures me.

"And, honey," Má says, "tell her face-to-face. It's better that way, not over the phone."

So when we get back to the house, I head up to my room, send Lee Lee a text, asking if she can come over because I need to talk to her about something. As I wait on her to reply, I get back into the usual routine of picking my clothes out for the school week and matching my shoes with them. I hang the clothes on my closet door on the latch thang. Then I go downstairs to see what Má is cooking up, and the doorbell rings. I open it, and it's Lee Lee.

"Hey, chick! Wuz up?"

"Let's go to the porch." I close the door behind me.

"No problem," Lee says as she sits down on the porch.

"Sooo, wuz up? You look really nerves."

"I am, ummmm, I don't know how to say this, so I'm just going to come right out and say it."

Lee looks for bewildered.

"Ty asked me out on a date with him. Before I knew it, I replied with a yes, not really thinking about, but then afterwards I reread everything, and I was like 'Oh my what have I done? What will Lee think?'"

"You know I really like Tyler." She looks over at me with no sincerity.

"Yes," I say, not sure what else will come out of her mouth.

"I think you should tell him that you're not going with him." Lee Lee folds her arms.

"I already told him that I would." I look over at her with a slightly leaned head.

"Well, cancel!" Lee shouldered up an attitude.

"Why would I do that?" I questioned.

"Because we are friends, and the code is, with gurl friends, that you are not supposed to even look at a guy I like." Lee rolls her neck.

"What code is this, and why am I just hearing about it?" My voice raise a bit.

"It's an unspoken code." Lee gives me the look like I should know this already.

"Until you just spoke it?" I say with full annoyance. "I'm not going to cancel because I already told him that I would go."

"But I like Tyler a lot, Carmella." Lee sounds pleadingly.

Before I knew it, I finally said it out loud, "Yeah me too."

"You never said anything before." Lee looks at me like I'm lying to her.

"No," I say, unbothered.

"And why not?" Lee starts yelling.

"Because you started showing how much you liked him. Really liked him. At first I thought you was just playing around, and then once you didn't stop, I knew you was serious. So I was just going to let yawl do yawl thang. Then Ty said that he didn't like you like that, and he meant it. I was like kool, okay. I didn't realize my feelings for him until he asked me out. I have been battling with myself to tell you."

"Like I said, if you was a true friend, you would cancel. If you don't, we want be friends anymore." Lee walks off the porch and heads home.

I sat there and watched her walk away in disbelief. Like really, she is going to not be friends anymore because I like Ty too and just never said anything to protect her feelings. He doesn't even like her. I spoke my truth and explained everything to her. Is she serious right now?

As I'm thinking all this, Má comes out to let me know that lunch is ready. She grabs my cheek. "Oh sweetheart, I see it didn't go so well."

"No. Lee told me if I go out with Ty, her and I want be friends anymore, but, Má, that's not fair," I whine and make my way to the kitchen and have a seat on the stool. "I was honest with her," I said, all confused.

"At times, that's all you can do." Má hugs me tight. "She will get over it. Friends have disagreements all the time. Just give her time."

"So you are saying I should go out with Ty?" I ask, looking for agreement.

"Now how you get that from what I just said?" Má asked. "It seems to me you have already made your decision. I told you to give Lee Lee time?"

"Okay, Má." I take a bite of my hawaiian roll sandwich.

"You don't understand it all right now in this sec, in this moment, but it all will become clear. What's going to hurt with just one date, huh?" Má comes and sit next to me.

I shrug my shoulders, take a bite of the pickle, and think, *It hurt Lee.*

After my shower, I began to pray. I'm on my knees beside my bed. *Lord God, I need your help. You know my situation with Lee and the Friday date with Ty. I still want Lee in my life. She is one of my best friends. Please help her to see this and that I truly apologize for any hurt I have caused her. In Jesus's name, Amen.* I get in my bed with a broken heart of friendship, then off to dreamland I go.

# CHAPTER 5

WEDNESDAY ROLLS AROUND, AND I look at my hands—manicure so needed. I'm wiping the tables down at work. Lee hasn't spoken to me. I tried talking to her, and she ignored me. So I will do as Má says to give her time, but it so hurts in the process. As I'm just about done with cleaning all the tables when Mo'Lynn walks in.

"Hey, gurl, how you been?" She throws her hand up like we are really that cool.

"I'm kool, what about you?" I said, still wiping.

She moves closer to me. "Why you and Lee Lee not speaking?"

I look over at her. "That's a private matter I rather not discuss."

"Oh, so it's like that." She began to walk to the counter to place her order.

"No, it's just...it's private is all. And where have you been? I have been seeing you at school, but you haven't been around. What's up with that?" I said as I finished the last table.

"I have been seeing my counselor a lot more. Just been having things going on in this head of mine."

I just look at her and say nothing.

"I'm going to order me a burger and let you get back to work." She begins to order.

I stare at her and then remember I don't have her number, which is why I didn't invite her on last Saturday. We still haven't finished understanding what really happened to Joz and where she was when it all went down awhile back.

I put the bucket and wash towels in the back and get the mop, broom, and squeezie to mop the floor. As I came out the closet, I see

Mo' at a booth. "I never got your number," I say as I'm dipping the mop into the bucket.

"Oh yeah, I don't have a phone per se. I have one, I mean it's a house phone." She takes some fries to her mouth.

"Can I have that then?" I reach into my pants pocket to get my phone out.

She give me their house number. I let her know that I will call her when the gang gets together. She says, "Kool." I finish cleaning the floor, and the next thing I know, it's time to clock out and go home. I didn't even see Mo' leave. I send a text to Joz before I clocked out to let her know the info I just got. I clock out, look over, and see Má is waiting for me in the car. As I walk out to the car, I'm thinking, *Soon I will have my own G-ride.*

"Hey Má," I say as I get into the front seat.

"Hey, sweetheart, so how was work?" Má says as I shut my door.

"It was good. Mo' came by." I buckle my seatbelt safety first.

"Mo?" Má raises an eyebrow.

"Mo'Lynn, Má," I say with a smirk.

"Oh, okay. So what happen?" She puts the car in gear and drive out of the parking lot.

"Nothing much. We was just talking about this and that."

Má keeps her eyes on the road. I look down at my phone to see if Joz has replied, and she hasn't.

The drive was pretty much silent on the way home. I really just looked at the streetlights and listened to the cars as we passed by them.

"Do you want to listen to some music?" Má reaches to turn the tunes on.

"Na, I'm good," I say, still looking out the window.

We make it into the driveway of our home I get out and go inside. As I open the door, Dad's voice sounds. "Hey there, how was work?"

"It was kool. Mo came by." I shut the door after Má comes in.

"Mo?" Dad question.

"Mo'Lynn, Dad. Mo'Lynn," I say as if I'm annoyed that my parents can't catch on.

Dad laughs and say, "How is she?"

"She is fine from what I could see. I asked her for her phone number because I didn't have it, and since she is in the group with us, I figure I could let her know when we all hang out," I say as I head upstairs.

"Good for you." Dad looks back at the TV.

Má chimes in. "So how did it go?"

"Má, I told ya what's what. I'm going to head to bed. Thanks for picking me up."

"That's what I'm here for and so much more." I hear Má say as I make it to my room.

I get my things to take a shower. All the while I was thinking something was really off tonight with Mo'. Something just wasn't right. I get out the shower get my pj's on and settle into bed. By this time, my phone is buzzing. It's Joz; she finally got back to me. CALL ME WHEN YOU GET THIS, Joz says in the text.

"Hey, wuz up?"

Before I could go on, Joz interrupts. "So tell me everything."

"I was cleaning for the night didn't even notice Mo come in. So we talked. She don't have a cell phone, just a house phone."

"Do people even have those anymore?" Joz chuckled a bit.

"I guess so." I continue, "I went to put everything away from when I was cleaning, and Mo' was gone. She ordered her food, ate, we talked, not that long, then she was gone. She didn't say bye are nothing."

"I told you it's something weird about her," Joz says. "Very weird, and I'm going to get to the bottom of it. Stuff is not adding up." I can tell she is thinking a lot more.

"I was thinking of inviting Mo to youth group. Just so we can get to know her more, help her feel more welcome," I explain.

"You welcome her your way, I will welcome her mine." Joz has attitude.

I think to myself, *Whatever.*

"I will see you at school. I need to find out more about this chick." Joz hangs up.

I look at the phone. "See ya."

I thought to call Lee, but I began to get sad and think about what's going on with us. I so wanted to tell her about my day, work at that, and everything, but she's not talking to me right now.

Just then I get a text from Ty. SATURDAY ALL DAY BE FREE. I WILL BE THERE TO PICK YOU UP AT NOON, IS THAT COOL? I smile as I texted back yes. I sit and look out the window as I lie in bed. What will come out of all this? I hope this doesn't mess up our friendship because of the date on Saturday. It has never really been just Ty and I. When we are with everyone else, we have a great time, but what will it be like just the two of us together?

I must had been thinking so hard that I fell asleep, and the next morning I heard my alarm. I really don't want to go to school today. I have to, so it ain't no point in thinking on that.

Ty is at the bus stop as usual. "Good morning." He looks at me.

"Morning," I muster up.

It's just something about him. I'm like, do I like him really? Have I always liked him and never paid attention? That's what I told Lee anyway. We have reached Lee's bus stop. She gets on and sits in the back, far away from us. She don't even speak.

Ty says, "Hey, Lee, you good?"

"Really, you going to ask me that?" she snaps with an attitude and roll her eyes.

He looks at me and says, "Wuz up with your gurl?"

"I told her that you asked me out on a date." I look down at my book bag.

"Okay. What's the problem?" He moves closer to the seat right next to me.

"Ty, really…" I look at him. "You know Lee has big crush on you."

He looks a little sad 'cause he has realized what's really going on. "Well, I don't like her like that. She is kool and all, but as a friend only. I only like you like that."

I blush and smile 'cause I know he is being so honest right now. In the back of my mind and heart, I still feel bad for Lee. As weird as it is, I don't feel as if I'm doing anything wrong. Lee doesn't even sit with us at lunch. By now everyone knows what's going on.

"Ty didn't like Lee Lee like that. We all knew it." Shareé takes a bite of her apple.

"Don't feel bad, gurl. Go on that date. See what it's like," Shará says.

"I totally agree." Joz does a quick look up from her phone.

Mo' just looks with a blank stare.

"How have you been, Mo'?" Joz blurts out, which I'm kool with because now the focus is no longer on myself and Ty; it's on to someone else.

"I've been good." Mo' look so uninterested.

"Have you heard anything about what happened in the locker room?" Joz asked.

"Nope." Mo' looks Joz straight on.

"Did you see anyone are anything funny like?" Joz points her phone at Mo'.

"Naw, not that I remember." Mo is so not for the convo.

"Well if you hear are remember anything, get at us." Joz throws her tray away.

The bells rings, and Mo' says on her way out, "I will see yawl lata." Under her breath, she murmurs, "Yawl are not going to find out that it was me, so just let it go. I'm still not done with her. She will learn to leave people alone. She wants to play, we will play."

The school day is over, and the weekend is right around the corner. I'm thinking as I'm getting on the bus. I see Lee getting on the bus. I smile at her, but she says nothing and goes to her seat.

As I walk through the door, Má shouts from the kitchen, "Hey, baby cakes, how was school?"

As I'm walking to the kitchen, I throw my backpack on the stairs. "Má, Lee didn't talk to me at all. She seen me on the bus, she didn't seat with us at lunch, she didn't wouldn't even talk to me in homeroom." I look and say with sad eyes. "I know what you said, give her time, but it's hard when I want to talk to her, and she act like I'm not even there." I sigh, looking down at my nails.

"Her time is her time," Má says, "and her way. Do you want to go out with Ty?"

"I didn't say that. I don't feel bad about it, either." I sat on the stool.

"Like I say, Lee Lee will be fine. Give her time. Her way, not yours. She will come around," she replies as she stirs whatever is in the skillet.

"Sure, Má," I say as I take a cookie and watch her finish up dinner.

# CHAPTER 6

SATURDAY, YOU ARE HERE. Ty sent me a message, told me to be ready after breakfast. I'm in the closet trying to find something to wear because he said it was a surprise. Boz don't know you can't tell a gurl to just wear whatever when we don't know where we are going! I see what I will put on my jeans outfit—my half-shirt that says GORGEOUS on the front with my wedge tennis. Yes, that should go fine. I'm just about fully ready, and I hear the doorbell ring. Má yells up the stairs, "Carmella, Tyler is here. I shout as I'm coming out my room, "Coming!"

"Hey." Ty stands there with a huge smile on his face. "You ready?"

I reach for my backpack purse. "Ready as I can be since you want to surprise me. See you lata, Má." I shut the door.

Since neither of us have a license (but I'm soon to get one), Ty's dad will be our chauffeur for the day. Ty opens my door for me. I get in the car.

"Hello, Sr."

"Hey there, Carmella, how are you?"

"I'm good."

He smiles. Ty gets in on the left side in the back to sit with me. "We ready to go?" Sr. ask.

"Yes, Dad." Ty touches the back of Sr.'s seat.

We drive out of the driveway on our way to everyone knows but me. I chill and look over at Ty. He is looking at me totally different now. I must say I like it. It's warm, honest, and adorable.

59

"Sooo are you going to tell me where we are going." I look over at Ty.

"Nope." He's playing the game on his phone.

"And why not?" I tap his shoulder.

"Because it's a surprise." He doesn't look up from his phone.

"Okay, surprise." I look back out the window.

We pull up to this ranch. It's breathtaking. They have the greenest grass I have ever seen. Long wooden fence. Beautiful apple trees as we keep driving on the dirt road. We pull up to what looks like a restaurant, but as we get out the car and start walking up, it's a house—big, huge lodge.

A young lady greets at the door. "Come right on in. I will show you guys the property grounds and then where we will serve you a late lunch," the host says.

Ty looks back and tells Sr., "We are good now, Dad. You know what time to be back?"

Sr. pops his head up and drives off.

We walk through this pretty pearl tile floors with sprinkles of gold and silver straight out to these huge double doors, down the stairs. I could see from where we are horses—Clydesdale horses. They are so beautiful. I look over at Ty and say, "Are you kidding me. How did you know?"

"You told me years back when we was in like fourth grade. You had Clydesdale everything. Backpack, pencil case, and binder. You haven't talked about them in a while so I thought I would surprise you with a ride." Ty looks like he know he has done well.

"Don't play with me. We can ride them?" I ask in excitement. "Oh yeah, it's a whole tour-type thang." Ty pops his collar.

We walk out to three horses. I pet the black one. Her hair is long and silky. Looks like her hooves are shoes, but it's just all her hair. The tour guide goes over the instructions on how to get on the horses, how we should not walk behind the horse, how to hold the rains, on and on and on. I was ready to get going. I'm so excited I can hear her, but I'm not listening. We all mount up on the horse, and on our way we go. We go into this beautiful field with daisy, sunflowers, and a hint of white lilies.

We keep riding until we get to a nice picnic area all set out for us to chaw down. We get off the horses, and there is so many snegatee snacks and grilled burgers with cheese, extra pickles, ketchup, and secret sauce. There are Icees in the cooler thingy and frenchie fries. Ty has really outdone himself.

So we sit and begin to eat, and there he goes again with his staring.

"What is it, Ty?" I say as I catch the food coming out my mouth.

"What do you mean?" His eyes are smiling.

"Why you looking at me like that?" I sip my Icee.

"Like what?" He bites his burger.

"Like you have something to say but—"

"But what?" He eats a grape.

"I don't know. You tell me. You the one looking." I point at him.

"I just have always had a crush on you." He looks down.

"What?" I had to cough.

"Don't act like you didn't know." He gives me that look.

"To be honest, I didn't." I look with my lips stuck out.

"So you never thought about it?" He gives me the be honest look.

"Huh… I mean yes, I like you. We have a great friendship." I reach behind me.

"You never looked at me then more than just a friend." He sips his ices.

"Not really. Then you asked me out. Then the thought came to me. I guess I really didn't want to think about it." I look at my shoes, wiggling my feet.

"Why not? You know what type of guy I am." Ty is very persistent.

"You know what? Yes, I like you, Ty, but I don't want whatever this liking is to mess up our great friendship if we don't work out." There is a sadness in my voice.

"Don't even think like that. Besides, we can keep dating until we are ready to be serious." Ty assures me as he touches my hand and looks me straight in the eye. "We can take it as slow as you want."

I almost choked on my grape in my mouth as I'm sipping my ices. As I swallow, I smile at him and think he is more than liking me.

We finish out our ride on the grounds. Head back up to the house. This time, I didn't notice it, but we had been holding hands the whole time. We get to the car. Sr. is just smiling from ear to ear. Ty opens the door for me again, and then he gets in.

"So did yawl enjoy yourselves?" Sr. looks toward the backseats.

We look at each other, laugh a bit, and say yes. We are still holding hands. I just keep looking out the window taking it all in. I don't want to miss anything. I even wanted to remember the way this day smelled.

We arrive at my home. Ty gets out first, then he comes and opens my door. He reaches out to grab my hand to help me out the car. He walks me up to the door—yelp, still holding hands.

"We going to do this again?" Ty asked.

"You and me?" I say as I reach for the door.

"Who else would it be?" He place his hands in his pocket.

I shrug my shoulders. "I will let you know the next time we doing this again."

"Okay." He gives me a hug. The whole time I'm thinking, *Don't try to kiss me 'cause, oh no, not while your dad is watching*. We release the hug. He kisses me on my forehead and says, "I really had a great time." Then he gets in the front seat, and Sr. drives off.

I open the door go in the house. Má is in the kitchen, whipping up something good.

"Carmella is that you?"

"Yes Má," I say as I walk toward the kitchen.

"Come in here and tell me how things went," Má shouts from the kitchen with true excitement.

I smile as a grab the white-legged stool with the basic-khaki top. I plump myself down and begin to let Má know how things went with Ty. She is smiling with delights the whole time I'm telling her. She gives me a bowl of Chex Flex. It's cereal with popcorn, choco-lates, peanut-butter chips drizzled with caramel. She gives me a glass of tea, cold tea, to go with.

As Má sits next to me, I go on and on about the date. I pause for a few seconds to throw a handful of the Flex in my mouth. As I do so, Má says, "So you really, as the young peep's word, 'digging' Ty?"

I laugh. "Naw, Má its feeling Ty. Yes, I like him. I never seen this side of him. Sr., the whole time he was driving, he was smiling and stuff, like you have been since I walked backed in, Má."

"Wait now. Wait," she says. "Before you jumping to anything, no, we didn't have anything to do with you too. But I will say I'm happy you two are feeling each other."

"Thanks, Má." I shake my head at her.

"You know I'm not just saying that, either. Your father and I want the best, very best for you to be your very best for yourself and whatever comes along." Má put some Flex in her mouth.

"I know, Má. I think I'm just going to have fun with it all and whatever happens will."

"I agree." Má says, kisses me on my forehead, and then we both clean the kitchen.

"Má, where is Dad?"

"He is working off site for the weekend. He will be back Monday."

I nod in acceptance. I head up to my room, still thinking of what a great time I had today. I want to call Lee, but I shut that thought down real fast. I checked my phone, and there was a text from the twins and Joz. So instead of texting them back, 'cause they all want to know what's going on, I just decide to call them—well Facetime all of them.

"Hey, girlies! Wuz up?" I bend my head a little bit.

"You know what's up. Stop playing and tell us all the juice." Shareé was twirling her finger around.

"It was really nice. I had never seen this side of Ty."

"Gurl, you smizing on Ty. Yawl going to go out again?" Joz asked.

"Yawl stop asking question and let C tell us what happen," Shará snaps.

"Well, hurry up because I got questions." Joz smacks her lips.

"Look we not about to do no questions want to be reporter. We just want the scoop." Shareé snaps her fingers.

"Okay, chill out!" I raise my voice. "He is Ty, but not like we see at school. I mean that's him too, but he is a gentleman."

"It sounds like someone has that L word that ends with an E in their future," Shará says with her head in her hands.

"I'll happy for yawl. That's really dope." Shareé looks closer in the phone.

Joz puts one eye up to the phone. "That's all kool and all, but when yawl going out again?"

"Don't know" I mimic her.

"Did yawl kiss?" Puckers her lips.

"Touch your nose. You know betta than that." I roll my eyes.

Shará chimes in. "You know good en smell well Carmella's a good gurl, and that's how she gone stay."

Shareé says, "Because you know if that was me, I would have kissed that face." She laughs a bit.

Joz says, "Just thirsty."

"Naw, that heffa is parched." Shará gestures with her hands. They all laugh.

I have gone on a daydream as I heard their laughter in the background. I'm somewhere totally different in my mind, just thinking what could be our name. *Will it be Tyella, C-Ty, Tymel? Naw.* I smile at my thoughts.

Then I hear Joz loud and too clearly. "Hey, chick, you still with us?"

"Naw, she gone." Shareé sings a little bit, and she can sing. "We about to get off the phone. We will get up with yawl tomorrow at youth group."

"I-ight. Kool," we all say in unison and hang up.

I lay on the bed looking at the ceiling are maybe not, still in my daydream.

My phone buzzed. It's a message from Ty. I wanted to read it, but I didn't. I told myself to go shower, get ready to journal and chillax, then read his text message. So after I get myself together, I sat in the wicker chair. I sat with my journal to tell of my day, and then I remember I didn't read the text from Ty. I grab my phone off the bed.

—HEY C JUST WANT TO LET YOU KNOW I HAD A GREAT TIME, AND
NEXT SATURDAY WE CAN DO IT AGAIN IF YOU LIKE.

—SO, YOU GOING TO TAKE ME AWAY EVERY WEEKEND?"

—THAT'S MY PLAN.

—I HAVE TO WORK SATURDAY FROM 9-6, BUT WE CAN HANG OUT
AFTERWARDS.

—KOOL. GOODNIGHT C.

I send back a sleeping funny pic.

I look out my window at the stars, just staring, thinking of
everything and nothing. I went to let Má know I was about to head
to bed. "Okay, sweetness, blessed dreams and visions," she replied.

As I walk off, I see Má looking at something. I told myself I
would ask her about it tomorrow. To my room and once that head
hit the pillow, I was out like a candle blown out.

# CHAPTER 7

SUNDAY MORNING, O HOW you have come! I arise to shine so brightly this morning. I go to the closet and just stand there thinking what I am to wear. I still can't get yesterday off my mind. That was indeed a great time. As I kept those great memories of yesterday at the forefront of my mind, I start to look for my clothes. I'm not a skirt kind of gurl, but hey, I'm feeling new and refreshed, why not try it?

I pull out a pretty jean dress. It looks like a jean coat but with a pleated-skirt design. It stops right at the middle of my knee. Since "new and bright" has come to mind, I put on my yellow sneakers, throw on my yellow watch band. Oh, I need to brush my face and wash my teeth. I talk backward to myself so I can understand at times. After I leave the bathroom, I head downstairs. Má was in the kitchen, fixing a small breakfast. We try not to have anything to heavy on a Sunday morning.

"Good morning, Má!" I greeted as I rub the counter.

"Good morning, sugar! How did you sleep?" She places some toast in front of me. I just smile. "I see that you are bright this morning. Is that a skirt you have on?" Má sounds very sarcastic. She sips her tea.

"It's a dress." I smile.

"Well, well, well." Má takes another sip.

"Sooo where's Dad?" I take a bit of toast.

"He will be home Monday. He is out on drill."

"Oh," I say. I don't think nothing of it because Dad is home sometimes, then he isn't.

After I have had my sugar bread, which is really cinnamon and butter, and Má' has finished her tea, we head to the car so we can go to service.

We pull up to service. I head to youth group, and Má goes where she goes. Just as I smile at Má and we each head to our direction, it's so funny I smell Ty coming up. I don't say anything. I never even paid attention to his smell before—or did I? He comes up and gently touches my shoulder. "Hey C." I look at him and just smile.

We head to youth group together. As we walk in, the twins are smiling too. We sit next to them. Shará gives me that "You go gurl" look. I smile, then I hear Mz. Cy'Queita.

"I'm going to need every one's undivided attention. Today's message is on boundaries—in other words, self-control. What do these words mean to you?"

Mo'Lynn raises her hand.

"Yes, go ahead," Mz. Cy'Queita instructs.

"Self-control means when you have that urge to do something that's not right, even those thoughts don't act on either one."

"Okay, that's good." Mz. Cy'Queita looks up at her.

"And boundaries are when you have respect for yourself and the other person."

"Mo'Lynn, those are really good personal definitions. Do you follow these?" Mz. Cy'Queita asked.

"To be honest"—Mo' drops her shoulders—"I try my best too, but sometimes, most times, I find myself fulfilling that urge and disrespecting those boundaries," she says with a sense of relief in her voice.

"Is there anyone else that has are might still be in the same shoes as Mo'Lynn?" Mz. Cy'Queita asked.

Everyone in the class rose their hands up.

"See, even when we think we are alone in our boundaries and no self-control, we are not."

I realized there are those times in my life, and I raised my hand too.

"There are times when we need someone who has overcome the obstacle that we a' dealing with at this time and season to help

67

us out. Hold us accountable. I would like for you guys to think on that for a moment. Be very honest. Who is that person that can hold you accountable, and are you a person that can hold someone accountable?

"Think on that, then when you get time, go to that person and let them know that you would like them to hold you accountable for this week. Seven days until we come back to meet again next week Sunday," Mz. Cy'Queita informed us all.

One of the youth said, "So that means we have homework?" he said with a snig of assurance in his voice.

"Yes," Mz. Cy'Queita said. "Hearing the Word with no application is irrelevant. If you truly believe the Word and what's being taught, then you will get the understanding and apply it to your life, where it can be applied. Does that make sense to you?"

"Once you put it that way that way, Teach, yeah, I get it," the youth replies.

Mz. Cy'Queita smiled. We got a fifteen-minute break, then the youth minister came in, brought a similar word to what Mz. Cy'Queita said. He was coming from Deuteronomy 19:14 from the KJV. Some of us youth like to read from other versions to get a better understanding. We keep telling the youth minister he is old school. He laughs at us. We teach him some of the new school lingo and thangs.

After service let out for everyone, I sat on the steps with Ty and wait for Má to come out. We really are not saying much, but chilling together is kool too. We just keep looking at each other, laughing and then looking away. By the third repeat of that, Má, Mrs. Claretha, and Sr. is walking out together.

"So yawl ready?" I say to Má.

"Yes, sweet love, home we go." Má reaches in her purse to get her keys.

"Well," Mrs. Claretha starts to say, "would you guys like to come over for lunch and relax a bit?"

Before we could respond, Ty placed his arm around my shoulders, looked at me, and said, "That would be kool" in a flirty, happy way.

I look at Má as I stand up and dust whatever is on me from sitting on the concrete steps. Má said, "Yes, we can come over. We will just follow you guys."

Ty says, "Why follow? If it's okay, I can just ride with you and get to the house."

"Good one, Son, but they know where we live," Sr. says as he agreeably taps Ty shoulder with a punch.

Mrs. Claretha says, "It's ok with me if its okay with Carmel that you ride with them."

We both look at Má. "Yes," she says as she looks back at us.

We all head to our cars. Ty opens the door for Má and me. He gets in the back with me, and we head to his house.

We pull up to Ty's house. We all get out and take a seat in the living area. Mrs. Claretha brings in little finger foods while her chicken, rice, and veggies are being warmed up.

As Mrs. Claretha sat down, she asked, "What would you kids be doing for Halloween this year?"

I take a bite of the snacks. "I didn't think much of it."

Ty states, "There is a Halloween dance next Saturday, C. You want to go with?"

"I have to work 'til six. What time is the dance?" I look at Ty.

He responded, "It's 7:30 p.m., I think. I can get tickets and everything, also pick you up. I will even get our costumes. What you think?" You can tell that he is already thinking of what to come up with.

"Now when it comes to costumes, Ty is your guy," Sr. says as he winks his left eye.

"Má, is it okay if I go?" I asked Má.

"I think it's fine. I will talk it over with your dad when he gets home tomorrow."

"Well, Ty, for now we are going. You know we have to have the best costumes, something that no one else will ever think to have. Can you do that?" I pointed at him.

"Most def. Just wait and see," Ty says with excitement.

Ty and I are brainstorming how *lit* it all will be. We must've gotten so indulged that the next thing we hear is Mrs. Claretha say, "It's time to eat, kiddos."

We all head to the dining room table. We take our seats, say our grace, and dig in.

"This is really slamming," I say. "Yes, it's very good, bae. You did really good." Sr. smacks.

"Thank ya. You know I had to be on point, got Mrs. Chef gracing the table." She smiles.

"Don't you start." Má points her fork at Mrs. Claretha.

"Lady, you know you can burn in the kitchen." She takes a bite.

"Yeah and you too," Má' says as she tilts her head.

They both began to laugh together, like they knew something we didn't.

Once we finish eating, Ty and I clean off the table, do the dishes together, and head into the living area, where our parents are drinking tea. Sr. is in his man cave watching the game. We head outside to sit on the porch. Nice day to be out—not too hot, not too cold. That's just right, whether the seasons are changing. Yeah, that's it.

We sat and talked about this, about that, then I see Má come out the house.

"Sweetness, it's time to go," Má says.

"Already?" Ty says with a bit of sadness in his voice.

Má smiles. "Yes. You can always talk on the phone. You teens know how to—how yawl say it—chat."

"Yeah, we do. Thanks for coming through. It was really kool." Ty grabs my hand to help me up.

"No problem," I say and give him a hug. He walks us to the car, opens both our doors, shuts them, then we are headed to our house.

On the road, Má says, "Ty is a really nice young man. He is being raised right." Má taps the steering wheel. I just smile at Má, thinking, *I'm so happy you approve.*

As we pull up to the house, Dad is chillin' on the porch. I jump out the car.

"Dad, I thought you wouldn't be back until tomorrow."

Dad just smiles. Má parks the car and hugs Dad and say, "It's so great to see ya." They kiss as old folks do and head into the house. "You're hungry, love?" Má places her purse and jacket on the hook.

"Naw, I made a sandwich," Dad says. They chillax on the couch.

I head up to my room and began to journal about my day. I love to sit and reflect on my day. As I'm writing, I stop in the middle, throw my pen and paper on the bed, and run downstairs.

"Má, did you remember to ask Dad" I say in a hurry

"About?" Má looks up at me from over Dad's arm with a puzzled look.

"Really, Má, you forgot already?" I look a little confused.

"Oh!" She laughs. "Ty would like to take Carmella to the Halloween dance Saturday. I said that it should be fine, but we will discuss it when you come home."

"Humm," Dad says, "you and Ty, huh?"

"Yeah, Daddy!" I look like "You already know."

"Naw, so I will say it again. You and Ty, huh?"

"Dad, really, what are you talking about?" I said. "Yes?" I flop on the couch.

"I'm talking about you and Ty. Since yawl went on that first date, you guys have been spending a lot of time together."

"I mean I guess you can say that." I sound so nervous.

"So you really like him?" Dad leans forward.

"Sure," I say, blushing.

My dad gives me a stern but playful look.

"Okay, Dad, yes, I like him." I gave out a sigh of relief, thinking to myself that's the first time I have said it out loud and really meant it.

"Not bad, C, not bad." Dad leans back in his recliner. "Well then, I say yes to you two going to the Halloween dance. You remember your curfew."

"Yeah, midnight." I get up from the couch. Má's mouth drops before she can say anything. I come out with, "Okay, 11:00 p.m." I put my hands under my cheeks and smile.

"That's a good time." Má looks me up and down.

I say thanks with as less excitement I could. Can't show my true excitement because I don't know where this is going with Ty. So I can't be all in like that. I have to take my time. I head upstairs to find my phone so I can let Ty know that it's a go for Saturday. After I text him, I finish journaling and just chill out for the rest of the night.

Another school week and I only work four days this week—Wednesdday, Thursday, Friday, and Saturday. That means it will be the one time I ever missed youth group. Man, so much I know that I will miss, but someone will let me in on the scoop.

Next thing I know, Saturdays rolls around. I'm halfway into my shift, and who comes through the door? It's Joz. Now she will fo' sho' let me know what happened on Wednesday.

"Hey, working gurl!" She holds the gurl a little too long.

"Very funny." I sit to eat my lunch. "What you doing here?" I place my food in front of me.

"I came to check up on ya see how you are doing." She sits across from me. "You been working and with Ty so much I hardly get to see my gurl." She takes one of my fries.

"Hushet, we see each other at school."

"Yeah, you right, but barely lunch, homeroom, first, third, and seventh periods ain't enough." Joz counted on her fingers. I give her a side lip tilt my head look, and we both start laughing. She digs into my fries and starts to yap about youth group. I say to myself, *Finally*.

"So the subject was on Halloween." She dips the fry in ranch sauce.

"What you mean?" I ask.

"Whether we shud celebrate it are not?"

"Huh. What are your thoughts on it?" I look as if why is there a problem anyway.

"I'll be honest, I don't have any. I guess I should, though, because it's a very important subject. What about you?" She is smacking on those fries.

"If we do the good with it all, it's fine." I take a bite of my burger. "I mean, just like it's kool that we are going to the Halloween dance. It's all in good fun, right?"

"Right," Joz agrees with a nod of her head.

"I wonder why it's so important to talk about?" I sip my soda water.

"I really don't know." Joz sounds so very uninterested.

"Are we planning to have something at youth group?" I reach for a fry, but there is none left.

"They haven't mentioned anything that I know of." Joz grabs her phone.

"You know we could throw something together." I nod, agreeing with myself.

"And when will you have time for that?" She gives me that look like "You already have enough on your plate."

"Forget it. My lunch is over anyway. I got to get back," I say with a 'tude.

"Wait." Joz grabs my hand as I get up holding the tray. "I still want to hear your idea maybe we can bring it up."

"I don't know." I move toward the trash can, put my tray at the top, go behind the counter to clock in, and begin to take orders.

That question is running around in my head. Why can't we celebrate Halloween? What's so bad about it? I'm going to ask Má about it when she picks me up. I know Lee and I are not talking, but I'm going to hit her up too. I just need different inputs. I know different cultures do different things. Got that because we have traveled some. Before I know it, my shift is over. I tell my manager good night and head out to the car.

"Hey, sweetheart, how was work?" Má is giving me the look, trying to figure out why I'm looking with my look as I'm getting in the car.

"Good. I got a question." I buckle my seatbelt.

"Okay." Má starts driving out the parking lot.

"Why does Halloween always come up with a question?"

"What do you mean?" Má can't look at me because she is driving.

"Like should we are should we not be doing it?" I look at Má, though.

"Carmella, don't get all worked up about it. If there is no conviction in your heart about celebrating Halloween, then enjoy yourself. If there is, then don't do it." Má has that straight-to-the-point voice.

"How do I know if my heart is being convicted?"

"Are your serious right now?" This time, she does look at me then right back to the road.

"Yes. Joz came by at lunch and was saying what was being discussed at youth group." As I'm talking, I can see Má being calm, her shoulders relaxed. "I was just wondering why it even has to come up. Why we can't just celebrate what we want and just be free?"

Má's smiles, touches my cheek with one hand while the other is on the steering wheel. "Questions will come up, sweetheart. That's how we learn. How you know what you know, and no one can change that. Only if you let them. You know right from wrong, and you know when your heart's being convicted. So what you need to do is chill out a bit. Do your research, and then come and let me know if you are still going to the dance three days from now." Má looks back at the road.

"I'm still going to the dance," I say with a little 'tude.

"Since you feel like that, then why bring the question up to even have the conversation?" Má snaps back.

I shrug my shoulders.

"So you want to know?" Má asked me.

"I will still dig a little deeper to see what I get."

"Good girl."

We pull up to the house, and it's smell so good as I pull the knob to the front door. Dad comes out the kitchen with his DADS ARE THE BEST CHEFS man apron on.

"So you at it again, ol' man?" I pat him on the shoulder.

"You betta know it." Dad gives the gesture. "Dinner will be ready to devour in a few minutes."

"So two minutes." I throw up two fingers.

"Don't be a smart butt. You know what I mean." Dad gives me that side look.

I smile and begin to set the table, thinking in my head, *Say what you mean what you say. I want ever say that out my mouth. I love my pretty whites.* Hahaha.

As I'm setting the table, I do remember that I have to finish my algebra homework. I meant to do it at lunch break, but Joz came in and got me all off. I will finish it. I don't have much to go, I mean left. I think maybe four problems left. So after dinner, I run up to my room finish my algebra, and then I check my phone. Got texts from everyone but Lee, which brought me to remember that I wanted to send her a text about Halloween. HEY LEE, IT'S CARMELLA. I HAVE A QUESTION ABOUT HALLOWEEN AND WHAT YOUR THOUGHTS ARE ABOUT IT? HIT ME UP WHEN YOU GET A CHANCE. I go and look at the other texts and reply. Pretty much everyone has the same question. What's up with Halloween?

So we all began texting on the group text. Even Lee Lee is involved in the text. We were discussing what we found out about Halloween and if there are things that we can change to make it betta for us. We are teenagers, but we are a strong group, and we know we have a voice. We all decided that we would take what we need from our research, what we see that was best for each of us.

Mo'Lynn came up with weird things, but we explained to her and showed her what we were talking about. She received, but you know she was still doing her crafts and spell and things. But step by step, we will all teach each other and show each other—hold each other accountable so we stay focused and on the right track. We all decided that we would be at the dance and have a great time. We were all going to make great memories. I love our group, I really do. We are all different and similar at times. But the differences is the beauty. *I love it!*

# CHAPTER 8

Ty HIT ME UP with a text about some ideas that he had for Saturday's dance—reality couples, future us, cartoon characters, and even transformers. I told him it doesn't matter as long as it's not anything scary, I trust him. I won't be at youth group on Wednesday because I have to work, so I let Ty know to just bring the costumes by Friday night or Saturday during the day. It will be here so that I can do what gurls do before a dance—be ready when he comes to pick me up.

Saturday rolls around. It was kool at work. Everyone showed up to the burger joint at different times. We chatted up a bit and told each other we would see each other later. Before I knew it, it was time to get off work. My parents are waiting outside to pick me up. I clock out and jump in the car. I'm so anxious that I forgot to say hi; instead, I tell my folks to hurry home as I have to get changed over.

"Excuse me, young lady, how was your day?" Má says.

"It was kool. Everyone came by. We talked about our costumes and how much fun we are going to have tonight. My apologies for not speaking when I got in the car."

"Sounds exciting." Dad puts the car in gear.

"Yeah, it will be!" I shout with excitement.

We head in the driveway. I jumped out the back seat before Dad stops the car, run into the house. I'm so anxious to see what costumes Ty has picked out. I run upstairs to my room, and there it is sitting on the bed. It looks like a cell phone. I'm thinking, *This is really lame. Who would want to be a cell phone?* Him being so teach savvy, this is what he came up with.

So yes, I'm so disappointed. I go to shower trying to find a way to make this costume kool because it's too late to change; he will be here in fifteen minutes. I put the costumes on, look in the mirror, and I mean, it's kind of cute. It has some shine on it, but really, how are we going to win best costumes in this? The next thing I know, Má is calling me down because Ty is here. I came down the stairs with the best smile I could muster up at the time, thinking to myself why I let him pick with no input. Goodness, I know for next time before I'll tell him, yes. I see Ty at the door in his costume as well. I'm thinking we look so lame. Má takes a pic of us, and we are out the door to the car, headed to the dance.

While in the car, Ty says, "So tell me what you think?" Sr. is up in the front, chuckling a bit.

"Why did you pick these?" I look at him after I look at the costumes up and down.

"I have some tricks up my sleeve, you will see." He has something in his hand.

"Okay, but my trust in you is wearing thin." I look out the car window.

"Just wait and see. You will like it." Ty is still messing with something in his hand.

We head into the school dance. The DJ got it popping in here. I'm enjoying the music so much I have forgotten about these lame costumes. The twins came checking us out. Shareé came as her favorite basketball player, Shará as her favorite model. Then comes Joz as a camera person with this, I guess, scary face. Lee is a comedian, Teli is an Avatar, and Mo' comes as a witch. I must say her costume is very nice—not so scary like I thought she would be.

She was whispering something as she walked around us before saying hi. I'm thinking to myself, *She betta not be trying to put no spell on us.* She is so weird and creepy at times. We all say hey and wuz-uppers and thangs. Then we hit the dance floor, doing every dance move known to us. We are getting it fo' sho'.

I shout out to Joz, "Hey, I'm going to get something to drink?"

"Okay, lightie, I will come with." Joz is laughing

"What you talking 'lightie'?" I look at her strangely.

"Your costume is lighting up like when we get a call on our phones." She points at me.

"Really?" I'm thinking it's still lame.

"Yeah, I know you think it's lame, but you have to admit it is cute, a really cute idea." Joz says, holding her cup up.

"Yeah, that should have stayed an idea."

We looked at each other and laugh as we pour our drinks from the punch bowl.

"I have to go to the restroom," I say as I sip my punch.

"You know I'm coming with you," Joz shouts over the music.

We head to the bathroom, and who's in there saying something strange we don't know? It was Mo'Lynn. She has a paper in one hand, some object in her other hand, looking at the paper, then the mirror, at the paper, then the mirror.

Joz screams at her, snatching the paper. "What are you doing?"

Mo' gives her this look like *Gurl?* She snatched the paper back. "I'm doing what I do. It's none of your business."

"You betta tell me are I'm going to get the chaperone." Joz was pointing in Mo's face.

"Go then!" Mo' shouts.

As Joz begin to head out, I grab her hand. "You not leaving me." I give her the big-eye look.

We head out to find a chaperone, and once we did, we let them know what was going on. We all head to the bathroom, but Mo'Lynn is gone. I remember I still have to pee. I'm scared so I ask them to stay in the bathroom with me until I'm done. I'm so scared and don't know what Mo' was saying and doing here. We leave the bathroom. The chaperone is one of the teachers; she said she will handle it at school on Monday. We go back to the dance. I'm still in shock. But no one really knows what happened, and as I look around the gym, I don't see Mo' at all anymore.

The dance is over. We all start to head home. I'm thinking how I am going to tell Má about this. She is going to ask about the dance. It was a lot of fun until the bathroom situation. We get to my home. Ty open's the car door and walks me to my front door. "I had a good time with ya."

"Yeah, me too."

We hug then I go in the house. The party was so good that I totally forgot about the lame costumes.

"So did you have fun tonight?" Má asked as she and Dad chillax on the couch.

"Yelp, it was kool. Good night."

They both turn back to the TV, and I head upstairs, get ready for bed. I grab my journal, begin to write, then there is a text. There is no number or name but a message that says IT'S NOT OVER! and that's it. I really don't pay it much mind. But mindful enough to where I don't finish my writing, I send the text over to Joz. She said she got the same one. So now we are thinking it must be coming from Mo', but how because she doesn't have a cell phone?

Joz says, SHE DOES HAVE A COMPUTER. ARE SHE DOES HAVE A PHONE AND DON'T WANT US TO HAVE THE NUMBER?

—WE WILL SEE HER TOMORROW AND HANDLE UP ON THIS.

—GOOD NITE!

—GOOD NITE.

Over at Mo'Lynn's house, she is fired up. "Don't know why those two came and messed up my whole plan. This would have been the perfect night to try my spell out. It's all good. It's not over and I will get my chance again. I know they will come get me tomorrow, and I'm ready for those heffas."

Sunday morning, I question myself, *Am I ready?* I can smell what Má is whipping up—some grits with cheese, eggs, french toast, and smoked sausage. I think to myself, *Wow, Má can really throw down in the kitchen.* I head straight downstairs to set the table.

"Good morning, sweetness," Má says without even turning around.

"How do you do that?" I look at her back.

"Because I'm supposed too." I can hear the smile in her voice.

As I'm setting the table, Dad comes down taps me on the shoulder, and says, "God morning."

I smile. He is already fully dressed. He goes in the kitchen, kisses Má, then starts to bring the food to the table.

We all sat down and began to eat. I devour mine, drink my orange juice, then head back upstairs to get myself ready for youth group. I'm thinking the whole time while getting ready what's going to be said and happen today with Mo'. She was really acting strange.

We get to youth group, and Mz. Cy'Queita and the twins are not here at all. We all look at each other like *Okay, who will be over group today?*

The youth pastor comes and says we are going to do things a little different today. "You group—correction, some of you guys have been coming here since youth group started. What I would like is for you all to pair up with someone that is new are that's not been here, but yawl really don't know each other, and we are going to talk and put into action the word 'relationship.' I want you guys to define what the word means to each of you, find scripture, give a scenario, and then show us how to apply. This is a new season, and its time we start to apply what we are learning. Look for the opportunity to apply. Be ready, willing, and prepared when it's time to apply. Amen."

So we all look at one another. I was thinking I would go to Mo'Lynn and really see what's up with her, but before I could get to her, Joz had already grab her. Goodness! I smack my lips. So as I look around, everyone was already paired up except Lee Lee.

So I go over to her and say, "The dynamic duo is back again."

She looks at me with a half-smile and say, "Not really."

So we sat down and began to work. As we are working, I'm starting to see and understand how she views our relationship and where I see our differences.

"Lee, we still can be friends. Just because we had one hick up doesn't mean our friendship has to end. I really miss you." I place my hands close together.

"How do you think I feel with seeing you with the guy that I wanted to be with. Marry even?" She gives me this really sincere look.

"Let's be real here. Is that true are your truth? 'Cause Ty never liked you the way you liked him, and he expressed that to you. So you telling me because yawl feelings wasn't mutual, I have to miss out because you think you are missing out?"

She looks at me questioningly. "I didn't look at it like that. All I seen was that you took my man." She rubs her arm.

"But was he really your man?" I look at her.

"I wanted him to be." She whines a bit.

"But was he?" I ask.

"No, he wasn't but even now I still like him, and how am I supposed to be your best friend with still liking Tyler?"

"I don't know." I shrug my shoulders. "I guess that's something we will have to figure out together. If that's what you want," I say in hopefulness.

"Can I think on it a bit? To be honest, I miss you too, but it feels really strange me liking Ty and us still friends." Lee doesn't even look at me.

"So you saying we are back friends?" I try to say with a Kool voice.

Lee says, "Yeah I guess let's give it another try."

We hug each other, and I'm super excited that she is back in my life.

I look up and say, "We have so much to catch up on, and I have to tell you about Mo'Lynn. It's all so QRZ."

Pastor comes back in, asking us how things are going. He can see that this subject has already began a difference a change in relationships, starting up new ones, renewing old ones. Pastor looked at Lee Lee and me. Good thangs to come.

As we head out of youth group, I'm looking around for Joz to see how things went with Mo, but I don't see her anywhere. I think to text her, but I don't have my phone. *Ugh!* I scream in my head. Service is over, we get in the car low, and behold, there is my phone just chillin' on the seat. I text Joz, HEY WHAT HAPPEN I DIDN'T SEE YOU AFTER YOUTH GROUP?

As my parents get in the car, they let me know that we are going to the Fishers for food and fun. I'm thinking that's great 'cause then I can just talk to Joz and see what's up. We stop by the house to get the delicious pound cake my Má makes, strawberries, and whip cream. I don't like whip cream. Then we head to the Fishers.

As we head in, Joz grabs my arm, and we went straight to her room. She shuts the door. We sit on her bed, and then she begins. "C, where do I start?"

"Start from the beginning, and don't talk too fast like you usually do when you are all excited."

"Okay, okay. Well, we sat down, and she don't hold nothing back. She goes right in about the Halloween dance at school and how we interrupted her from what she thinks is important and how we need to apologize."

"Apologize for what?" I say with disgust.

"Let me finishaaa."

"Uh-huh."

"Then she says that we betta be ready for what's coming."

"And what do she mean by that?" Now I'm ready to lay some hands.

"Don't know. It got me thinking that she is the one who sent us those text messages, but we have to prove it, just can't assume." Joz looks at her phone.

"What do you want to do?" I ask her.

"Still thinking on that. We should get the crew involved."

"Kool." I gave her a high five.

Joz sends a mass text to everyone as we head downstairs to eat.

"It's good to see you, ladies," Mrs. Fisher says with a chuckle.

We sneakily take our seats to eat. The food is great, by the way. Us youngsters clear the table and head outside on the front porch to read our text and see how to handle this Mo' chick.

As we are chillin', we receive another text from the unknown number. I HAVE WARNED YOU, it says. We both look at each other, and Joz says "Who do she think she is? She not scaring nobody. Oh, I got something for her."

"Like what?" I look at her like she knows she ain't going to do nothing.

"Oh, you just wait." She studies the text. Right as she finished, my parents came out to let me know that we were leaving. I look at Joz and tell her to keep me up to date because I know she will get to the bottom of this.

Once home, I go to my room, and this just came to mind—I should check on the twins. See where they were today. HEY CHICK-A-DEES, DIDN'T SEE YOU GUYS AT YOUTH GROUP. JUST WONDERING WUZ UP. HIT ME BACK WHEN YOU GET A CHANCE.

I sit in my window with my journal and write about today. There are thoughts running through my mind of what were we going to do about Mo'Lynn. No, we are not telling our parents—we can handle this on our own. *But* can we really?

# CHAPTER 9

WITH ALL THE THOUGHTS running around my head, before I know it, I'm being awakened by Má.

"Do you plan on being productive today?"

I look at her sleepily. "What's going on? What time is it?"

"Time for you to shine," Má says.

I try to muster up a smile, at the same time thinking to myself my Má can be so caring and sweet. I come to the realization it's past time for me to be at practice. I do have plenty of time to head to youth meeting to talk about the party for October.

Everyone shows up on time for the youth meeting. We all huddle up and begin to brainstorm and see what to come up with.

Mo' says, "What about a heaven-and-hell party?"

"What is that?" Joz says.

"My mom used to have them all the time at her house doing Halloween. She would divide the living room into two sections. One side would be heaven, the other side hell. It would cost two dollars to get to each side each time you want to get in. Everything in heaven was nice, cool, and sweet. Hell was hot, spicy, and did I mention hot."

I'm thinking, as Mo' is going on, *I thought she told me she didn't meet her mom are something like she didn't see her till she was three are something?* Her story never adds up, but okay then. "Anyone have any ideas what can be put in each side? Where we want it and what kind of decorations, food, and everything. Really good idea, Mo." I look at everyone with my pad in hand.

So as everything is coming along, we then let the youth pastor know and it's a go. He reminded us not to forget a cleanup crew. The gym needs to look the way it was before the party.

Since Joz is all about news and spreading the word, she gets right on making flyers with Ty, and then she starts posting to everyone she knows and tagging us all in them on social media. Mo', Lee, and I work on what decorations, food, and everything else we will need. We already know my Má will do all the cooking. I will ask her when she comes to pick me up. Lee said she would ask her mom.

I look at Mo' and say, "Hey, can you ask your mom since she has had these parties a lot?"

She looks at me with sad eyes and say, "Not going to happen, we don't know where she is."

"My apologies." I place my hand on her shoulder.

"No need, you didn't know." Then she just walks off like its nothing.

Telion and some other teens are just chillin' until we let them know what they will be doing. Actually, chillin' to them is playing b-ball, gurls versus boz. That's when I realize I don't see the twins. I also remember they didn't hit me back up when I texted them. So before everyone leaves, I let them know to be here Friday at 4:00 p.m. That gives us enough time to set up and still chillax before the party starts. Everyone shouted "Kool!" and left.

I hop in the car. "Má, can you make some sweet and hot foods for the heaven-and-hell party that we will have this Friday night at the church?"

"Sure, do you know what yawl would like?" It looks like Má is already starting to make a list in her head.

"Nope. I thought I would leave that up to you. Lee says that she will ask her mom too, so maybe yawl can get together and come up with a menu?"

"Yeah, it's been sometime since we cooked together. I will give her a call." As Má was talking, she got a text from Mrs. Leng, and they would have a gurls' time on Thursday night up until Friday, the time of the party.

"I'll ask Dad to see if he can deliver the food." I checked "asking Má" off my list.

"You sound like you know what you are doing." Má stops at the red light.

I look over and point my pen. "I learn from the best."

"Thanks, lovebug." Má winks at me.

I sit in the front seat still brainstorming and thinking there is a lot that goes into planning a party. *Goodness!*

We all get to the gym on Friday. We have some stragglers, but it's all good. Everyone gets moving and on their jobs. 'Bout time we are done, it doesn't look like a gym. We have divided the gym into two sections. The talent we have among us is like no other. The artistry gets you feeling like you are in heaven and hell for real. It's really kool, definitely getting pic for sho'.

So the party starts at 7:00 p.m. and ends at 10:00 p.m. Youth advisors are here to chaperone and make sure everything is in order. By 6:50 p.m., we have a huge line out the door. Ty and Teli is taking the money with help from within their sections. The food is banging. On the heaven's side, we have cupcakes, ice cream, fresh tea with lemon, Icee, cake, fruit, and candy apples. On the hell side, there are spicy nachos, hot donuts, hot soda, hotdogs, and a fire-pit-themed cake. Once everyone is inside, they are having a great time. So far, one kid ran out to get into the heaven line. His tongue was hanging out, trying to say, "Hell is too hot." We all laugh.

We did good on the party. Now it's cleanup time. Before we all start to clean, Joz runs into the gym, screaming, "Come to the bathroom! Mo'Lynn has collapsed!"

We all run without a thought. Ty and Teli, they don't move at all. One of the advisors was standing at the door and told us we couldn't go in.

"How are we going to know what is going on? Even to see if she is all right?" Joz insists, still trying to enter the bathroom. She goes so far to look under the advisor's arm. Lee and I look at her with the likeness of, *Is she serious? She don't even like the gurl. She just too dang nosy.*

The advisor and Mo' come out of the bathroom with Mo's arm around her shoulder. "She will be fine. We have called her grandparents. They are on their way to get her. Head back into the gym to finish the cleanup pls." We head back in the gym with the others to finish up on the cleaning. As Lee and Teli take the trash out, I stand at the door to watch, all the while thinking, *It's always something with Mo'*.

Parents have arrived to pick us all up, but we didn't notice because most of them were in the lounge with Mo' and her grandparents, being concerned, nosy, and seeing if there is anything they can do to help. As we meet our parents in the lounge area, I'm watching Mo' the whole time to see what's really up with her. Is she doing all this for attention.? Did something seriously happen to her? Is she okay? As I'm watching her, the dads are holding a convo with her grandfather.

This heffa begins to put a smirk on her face, like that "I got cha" type. I had to triple blink to make sure what I saw what I saw. I nudge Lee, and she whispers in my ear, "Yelp, I seen that too."

Joz comes out of nowhere. "Yeah, me too, and I'm about—"

As soon as she was about to move in and say something, Lee put her arm up in front of Joz's chest, looked at her, and say, "Oh we will get her. Bet that."

Joz stared back in agreement.

As we make it home, my Má is still talking about the situation from the party in full concern. My father goes to sit on the couch after coming out the kitchen with some hot chocolate for Má and I. "Honey, I see your concern, but you have to let her grandparents handle this and just be there for them. Can we talk about something else?"

"Oh please!" I interrupt with my eyes as big as I could get them.

"Why you say that like that, Carmella?" Má is serious.

"Because it seems every time we get together, she is up to something, and that's no good." At this point, I'm very aggravated as I start to explain all the events. "Think back to the get-together we had here, the Halloween party, now this party."

Má states, "I can see how things look, but if she needs help, then we should be there."

"You can't be there for someone who don't want you there," I say as I drink my hot chocolate with no marshmallows, thank you.

"Just be there when you can." Má gives me the "I'm not playing with you" look.

"On that note, ladies, we are going to call it a night." My dad reaches for Má's hand and head upstairs.

I grab my phone and began to text Joz and Lee just to see where their headspace is. No one replies as quick as I want them to, so I head upstairs, shower to get the night off then get in bed. No matter what I do, I can't sleep. Good thang, it's the weekend and I have nowhere to be tomorrow. I still can't sleep, so I check my phone, still no replies. I did not even realizing the time since I texted the twins to let them know what's was going on and ask where had they been. They have been missing in action without saying nothing to no one.

Saturday morning, you know I'm not ready for you! I'm so tired, really didn't get any sleep at all. To work I do have to go. I really thought I had nothing to do today. I clock in at work in a daze because I didn't get no sleep! On my lunch break, you wouldn't ever guess who shows up.

"You don't look to good, you 'ight?" someones said from behind me.

I look over my shoulder. "What are you doing here, Mo?"

"This is a public place. I come for burger and fries." She is walking to make her order.

"Really. All that drama you pulled last night, didn't think to see you at all."

"Now why would you say that?" You can tell Mo' is up to some mess. I give it to her—she wears that drama crown well. "Why are you bring up last night today is a whole new day." She looks back at me from the order counter.

"You really going to act like nothing happened?" I put a fry in my mouth.

"Yelp, let's leave it there in last night." Mo' grabs her food and takes a seat at a booth alone.

Before I could reply to her, Ty walks in. "Hey, ladies, how is it going? Mo'Lynn, you look a lot betta then last night." He was looking at both of us. I look at Mo' with one eyebrow up.

"Last night was last night. I really just want to leave it there, if you don't mind." Mo' sips her drink.

"Kool. C, you have time to eat lunch with me. I want to run something by you."

"Order and have a seat with me when you get your food."

Ty comes over with his food, and we start to chat it up. I say to myself, make a mental-note type thang, *Text Lee and Joz about this later.*

"I was wondering what you will be doing over the holidays," Ty asks.

"Which one are you talking about?" I look at him as I bite my burger.

"Either one." He dips his fry in his ranch sauce.

"Why? Wuz up?" I don't look up; I just keep eating—my lunch break won't be forever.

"Around Christmas and New Year's, my family goes up to the cabin to vacay for a bit. I thought I would get a head start and see if you and your fam would like to come with. It's really kool. I think you would like it."

"I will ask my parents and see what they say," I reply as I snatch one of his fries. "It's kind of early, but hey why not?"

We finish our lunch. Ty leaves, and back to work I go.

As my shift comes to an end, I remember to text Lee and Joz. I grab my phone and see that I have a text from the twins that says, WE WANT BE COMING BACK.

*Wait, what?* I'm in shock right now, my mouth all gaped open. I text back, WHAT'S UP? I look up, and Má is outside waiting on me.

I hop in the car in frantic mood and tell Má what the twins just texted me. "Have you heard from Mz. Cy'Queita?"

"Put your seatbelt on, calm down, and take a breath. To answer your question, yes, I have, but that's grown folks' business. You will have to get what's going on from the twins."

"Má, that's not telling me nothing, and neither are they," I say as I buckle my seat belt.

"It's their choice. Give them time." Má puts the car in gear.

"How am I to respond to what they text, "we not coming back'?"

"Like I said, sweetness, give them time." Má pulls out the parking lot, and we head home.

*I always have to give people time*, I think to myself.

I look at Má, and she knows what's up and she won't tell me. As I think about it, I get madder and madder. *Grown folks' business, huh?* But would she like that if I told her when she was in mine, "It's young folks' buziness!" I sit in the car quietly the rest of the way home because I'm so pissed I could spit.

# CHAPTER 10

AFTER WE MAKE IT home, I go straight up to my room. I send the twins a text and tell them that I don't understand and I'm here for them and that I will fo' sho' miss them. As I was texting the twins, I receive a text from Joz and Lee, just seeing how things went today. That's when I remembered about Mo' showing up.

In no time, Joz chimes in. "So you telling me that she is playing us?"

"Pretty much," I say.

"It took you that long to see, reporter?" Lee laughs. By this time, we are all on Facetime.

"Hush it!" Joz looks like she is slapping the phone.

"Something has to be done. It's always something with her," I suggested. I check to see if the twins have texted me back.

"Tru that, tru that," Lee said as she put some kind of fruit into her mouth. "So what's the plan you got, Joz?"

"I'm thinking we should plan a sleepover, but it be with the mothers too. So then everyone can see her for who she is."

"Great idea. We can include everyone. I will send a mass text." Lee is all excited.

"Don't send one to the twins," I snap. "Everyone that will be there is already on the call."

"Why we can't ask the twins?" Joz looks like *What is going on?*

"Because they not here no more," I reply with sadness all in my voice. "I sent them a text and they replied, 'We not coming back!'"

"Oh! Now I wonder what happen?" Joz looks as she is picking something out her eye.

"Well, get on it, reporter, and give us the scoop."

"Lee, stop being funny."

"Oh I'm not, but hey, that just gives you more practice for when you do become a reporter, right?" Lee sticks her tongue out.

"You right, you right." We can see Joz dancing around. "Then that means it will be me, you, Lee, Mo'Lynn, her grandmother, and our mothers."

I pop my head.

"Sounds about right to me," Lee agrees.

"Dang! I wish Mz. Cy'Queita and the twins could be there."

They reply in unison, "Me too…"

"Where and when do you plan on having this sleepover?" I ask Joz. "Let's strike while the pot is hot. This weekend coming up, no later than the one after that."

"How you going to get Mo'Lynn to come?" Lee asked Joz like *You know this just might not work.*

"Oh, watch and see me work!" Joz says with full confidence.

"Hey! Hey! Hey!" Lee snaps her fingers.

"See if its kool with your mom, Carmella, that we have it at yawl house since yawl have the bomb fire in the backyard. We can have all the moms and Mo'Lynn's grandmother do all the cooking for the weekend. Be like a potluck. I say we get together Sat around noon, then everyone leaves Sunday after breakfast." Joz is so on it today.

"Sounds like a plan!" Lee says.

"I will ask my Má tomorrow 'cause I'm mad at her right now."

"Why, man? Don't start messing up stuff." Joz is looking like *Please.*

"Because she knew the twins was gone and didn't say nothing. Going to tell me its grown folks' business."

They both laugh. "Well, your mom is right," Lee says with no feeling at all. "She doesn't talk to the twins, but she talks to Mz. Cy'Queita.

"I guess." I throw my shoulders up.

"Hey that's something else we can easy drop on the moms while they are talking about that because you know they are." Joz starts dancing again like she got it all figured out. "I will halla at yawl Lata" Lee hangs right up. We all disconnect from the facetime.

Sunday morning rolls around, and my folks are just chillin' on the couch. I run downstairs thinking I'm late for youth group, and as I'm about to hit the bottom step, Má says, "We not going, luv."

I look at her questioningly but ask really quick, "Can I see if Ty and his parents can swing by and get me?"

"Sure," Má says not even looking over the couch.

I call Ty, and he says sure, and before I know it, they are outside. I hop in the car, and we head off. "Good thang you called when you did because we was literally right down the street." Ty looks at me. I think to myself, *Just two years, I will have my license, then my car. Soon. Soon. Soon.*

After youth group, Ty and his fam drop me off. I head into the house to ask Má about the sleepover. She told me she had already started receiving calls and text from the other mothers. She added that Mo'Lynn's grandmother was coming this weekend and they were bringing their favorite cookies and tea.

"Oh, okay kool. Everyone is on it, huh?"

"Sure thang," Má says. "I think it will be a nice time, and all of us ladies can bond while yawl youngsters do whatever."

I take a handful of pork and a blanket then head to my room. Before I even get there, Joz is calling me. "Did you hear?" she says anxiously.

"You need to wait for me to say something before you just start talking." I try not to scream at her.

"Gurl, whatever. Lee is on the phone too, and did you hear?"

"Hear what?" I ask like I don't know what she is talking about, but I do.

"The sleepover is on." You can hear her smiling through the phone.

"Yeah, Má told me when I came home. You are super excited, huh?" I plump down on my bed.

"You know it! Like a cow in a cow patch!" Joz says.

Joz screams.

"You got the cow part, right?" Lee laughs too loud. I chuckled. That was funny.

Joz say, not laughing at all with us, "You a comedian now!" You can hear in her voice she is not kool with being called a cow.

"Could be. I got many hidden talents I'm discovering," Lee replies.

"Chil, bye." Joz laughed.

"Let's get back to the sleepover. Yawl want to wear onesies. We can order them and have them here in no time," I say.

"I already have the ones we got alike, so I'm good," Lee says, which means I'm not buying another one.

"I will have my mom get me one and will let Mo'Lynn know too," Joz says.

"Kool. So it's all good."

"Yelp."

Saturday rolls around, and everyone was at the house before noon. Dad was gone to drill for the weekend, though I already knew he didn't want to be home with cackling hens. This is about to be a great little shindig. Everyone is pretty much all over the place, hanging out, chillin'.

Joz gives me that look and us youngsters head out to the back porch while the moms chill inside. We are talking about everything and nothing, then Joz starts to go in on Mo'.

"So Mo'Lynn—"

Before she can finish the rest, Lee blurts out, "Let's play truth, dare, double dare, promise, are repeat." Then she gives Joz a look like *I just saved you—hope you are paying attention.*

Joz says, "Mo'Lynn, pick one."

"Oh, so I have to start first." Mo' looks at Joz like she is already getting on her nerves.

"Sure, why not?" Joz claps her hands.

"I will play the game, shoot," Mo' snaps. "I choose truth."

"Is it true that you always has something under your sleeve?" Joz asked.

"And like what?" Mo' looks as if, *Really.*

"Is it true are not?" Joz is getting testier this moment.

"Wait, like what?" Mo' asks like she didn't hear the question the first time.

"Just answer the question!" Joz folds her arms.

Mo' is looking really confused and uncertain if she should answer the question or not. She is mumbling something to herself, but we can't hear her. *Who do this gurl think she is? I'm not about to give up nothing. I have to stay on top of my game. I will give Joz what she wants alright,* Mo' says to herself.

"Maybe. Maybe not," Mo' says, smirking at Joz.

Lee states, "You can't say that. If it's true, you just say 'True.' If it's not, then you say 'Not true.'"

"It can be true, and it can cannot be true. It just all depends on the state I'm in are the results of a situation." Mo' looks like *Yelp got 'em.*

"Can you just answer the question? It's just a simple question, and you are just going around and round." Joz is past aggravation.

"It may be simple to you, but not me." Mo' is laughing on the inside at this point, and you can see it.

"I know what you are doing, and it's not working. So put it this way. With any recent situation, do you have something up your sleeve?" Joz look at Mo with her eyes popping out her head.

"Right now, ummmmm, nope." Mo' looks down and also says something, but we can't hear her. *If you were paying attention, you would see that I already showed you what was up my sleeve.* I look at Mo' and can tell she is lying. So we keep playing the game. The dares are the funniest because we figure out that trying to get the truth out of Mo' is not going to happen. She did find out some of our truths, so that will show her that she can trust us. But can she really?

"Chickadee's, I'm going to be right back." I go in, throwing the sliding door through the kitchen. I hear Má talking, and then I hear Mrs. Fisher. They all have their wine glasses looking so elegantly fun.

"Ladies, ladies, wait, I have to tell yawl something this is so embarassing, but I have to share it. Are maybe it's the wine that's making me say this." Mrs. Fisher takes a sip before continuing. "It's so funny. So while I was in the shower, shaving my armpit and trying to rinse myself off, 'cause we have that shower head that can detach. Honey, I got to my pocketbook. It started feeling too good, and before I knew it, I cut my nipple."

The mas all start cracking up laughing. One of them said, "Uhhhhhhhhhhh." I'm thinking to myself, *Man what have I walked into?* I walked past them to head to my room to get some board games, and they all got really quiet but still chuckling with their glasses up to their lips.

"Sweet love, you need something?" Má says as she is trying not to give them all away in her giddiness.

"No, just headed up to get some board games."

"Yawl good out there?" Mo'Lynn's grandmother says, threw a hiccup.

"Yes, thank you."

As I run upstairs, I hear Mrs. Fisher say, "I hope she didn't hear that." Then she burst out laughing even louder with the ladies.

As I head back down through the kitchen, the parents are still at it. They are having a great time, which is good—my Má needed this. She has been down a bit, and I don't know why. This weekend has brought her laughter and joy. I hope it stays this way.

"Hey, chicks, I got two board games." I can't believe no one is cold and ready to go in 'cause I'm both. I set the board games down.

"It's really nice out here. The stars are clear through the sky." Joz is looking up.

"Have you gurls ever wished on a star?" Lee asked because she probably already made her wish.

"I have," Mo' says, and she sounds excited.

"Did it come true?" Lee leans in to see if it did or didn't.

"Don't know yet," Mo' says, shrugging her shoulders.

"Why you just can't answer a question straight out?" Joz stands up and screams.

"I'm going to need you to get your chick." Mo' looks at me with her thumb pointing at Joz.

"Naw, I'm good. Yawl need to work this out." I leaned back in the wicker chair.

"Work what out?" Mo' still looks unbothered.

"U know what it is?" Joz snaps as she stands. "You have been messing with me since you got here. None of this stuff happened when you weren't here."

"What stuff are you talking about?" Mo' eats a grape.

"You know what I'm talking about." Joz rolls her eyes. Joz doesn't want to say it first because she wants Mo' to say it, because as she was asking Mo' about having something up her sleeve, she and Lee has something up theirs.

"Mo'Lynn, why you just can't be straight up with us? It's like you always hiding something," Lee asks.

"I don't trust as easy as some." Mo looks wide eyed at Lee.

"It's not about trust. Right now, it's about you owning up to your stuff."

"All of it!" Joz interrupts.

"Can you let me talk, please?" Lee snaps her head at Joz.

"Own up to what? Why would I? If I told ya you can't—what you going to do about it?" Mo' nut's up, and she has that look like *Yawl got me all the way bent.*

"We will know once you admit to it, Mo'Lynn." Lee looks at her like she not playing now.

"Why yawl think it's me?" Mo' looks at both of them.

"I just told you why." Joz gives her this look like *You know we know.* But Mo' looks back at her like *You think you know, but you don't have proof and if you think I'm going to give it to ya, you got life messed up.*

"Let's just let it go for now because this is getting nowhere," I say to all three of them as I throw my hands up.

"If you want us all to be friends, then you have to trust us, and we have to trust you," Lee insists.

"Who said I wanted us to be friends?" Mo' points her hands to herself and to Lee.

"If that's how you feel, why are you here?" Joz frowned.

"You really need to chill out. I'm just kidding. Like for real, stop being so serious all the time." Mo' sips her soda.

We all just sit by the bomb fire. It looks like everyone has questions dancing in their head.

Before I knew it, we all fell asleep by the fire. I get up to look around, and Mo' is not in her chair. *Goodness, where is this chick?* I wake the gurls up to show them that Mo' is gone. We quietly start to look for her. We are tiptoeing around our mas because they are laid out everywhere in the living room. We checked backrooms and every room in the house. We check the driveway. Then we head back to the backyard from the side gate. I look back and whisper, "Shh, I will latch it."

We look at each other, thinking where can this gurl be. Lee says, "We didn't check the garage." I'm thinking to myself, *She betta not be in there with the car on 'cause if she is, I'm going to kill her.*

We get to the garage, and she is sleeping in the old car my dad and I are fixing up when we get time here and there. My dad says I need to know how to fix most things on my car when I get it. I don't know why, but hey, I think it's a dad thing. It has been fun working with Daddy on the car. We are getting pretty. Before I could finish my thoughts, Joz says, "Look, she has a journal. We should read it."

Me, being the voice of reason, tried to stop her. "Would you want someone reading your personal stuff?"

Before she could respond, Lee took the journal out her hand and started reading it. She was reading fast, her eyes open super big. "We should put it back before she wakes up," I whisper. Lee puts her hand to quiet me. She puts the journal back, grabs my hand, and starts to run out the garage to the backyard. She is breathing really hard. Once we get back to the bomb fire, which is not on fire any-more, I begin to get it started back up, as Lee starts to talking.

"Mo'Lynn is really on something. Because all the horror and junk that she has in there," Lee says with this scared look on her face.

"You only read a couple of pages. What could you have really got in that short time?" Joz asked.

"Are you serious? As much as you want to be a reporter, you already know you don't need much for the truth." Lee is still shaking a bit.

"Okay, naw stay focused. What did you read?"

Before Lee could say anything, Joz blurts out, "We should have had our phones so you could have taken pictures. Now we want have no proof. It's your word against hers."

"You're right," Lee agrees as she is still taken a back.

"Let's go back in and get the proof." Joz starts to walk back to the garage. Right then, we hear something like someone is walking. We all look in the direction of the sound with suspense.

"Hey, what yawl doing up this early?" Mo' is holding her journal as she walks toward us.

"There goes our chance to get evidence," Joz mumbles and plumps down in the wicker chair.

"Where are you coming from?" I ask as if I don't already know.

"I went into the garage. I like to be alone when I write. You guys had fallen asleep. I went to find somewhere private." Mo' takes her seat.

"If we were asleep, why you just didn't write here? You had privacy." Joz looks.

"I thought I might wake you all, so I just went elsewhere."

"Uh-uh." Lee gives her a look like *I should tell on you.*

Before we knew it, the sun was up, and we could smell breakfast cooking. We all head into the kitchen. The moms were hooking it up. We had bacon, eggs, muffins, fruit, juice, and water. The parents had their mimosa.

"So, gurls, how was last night?" Mrs. Leng ask as she pours Mo' some juice.

"It was cool. I wish it wasn't ending today," Mo' answers.

"Hmm." Her grandmother looks at her. "It would be nice, but you know we have plans for later today."

"Yeah, plans I don't want." Mo' has an attitude.

"Young lady, we don't speak with that tone in my home to *no* adult. We always show respect," Má says as she places a waffle on Mo's plate and gives her that look like *You betta not let it happen again.*

"I apologize." Mo' looks at her grandmother.

"Accepted." Mo's grandmother winks. Má shakes her head.

We finish that good ol' breakfast, then we all help clean up. As we are just about finished, Mo's grandfather shows up to pick them up. As he stands at the door, he says, "It looks like yawl had a lovely time."

"It was so lovely I don't want to leave," Mo' says as she walks past her granddad. But before she could get all the way out the door, Má calls her out. "Mo'Lynn!"

She looks back at my ma.

"You forgot just that fast, huh?"

"My apologies, Mrs. Carmel."

"And?" Má looks at Mo'.

"I apologize, Grandpa."

"Now you have apologies twice. Let's work on it not happening again, okay?" Má gives Mo' that look like *You can do this.*

"Yes, ma'am."

Us gurls look at each other like *Really, she has respect.* So they head out, but Mrs. Leng and Mrs. Fisher are still here.

Má says, "Oh, I forgot to tell ya. We discussed it last night, and they all will leave tomorrow. The men are out fishing this weekend, so hey, they can stay."

"No problem I'm fine with it," I say, doing a little dance.

We all get ready for whatever day we are about to have. After we are done, it seems like they just love this bomb fire pit. Yes, it's cold. As we sit around to get warm with no shoes on, just really good thick, long socks, Joz tell Lee, "You need to write down everything you can remember from what you read out of Mo'Lynn's journal, and then we will keep it somewhere safe. Even though she said she was in the garage, what if she was walking around, snooping around the house? We don't know because we was sleep."

"You are so right, so right." Lee look over at Joz, all bundled up under her cozy blanket.

"I have a blank journal. We can just keep everything in there, and I will keep it in a safe place. We did have a good time in spite of drama queen." I cheesie real hard.

"Don't go there, it was my idea." Joz sips some hot chocolate.

"Yeah, might have been, but I executed it very well." I pat myself on the back.

"You both did great!" Lee jumps in.

We all laugh. I get up to get Lee the journal and a really cute pen to go with it. I hand it to her, and she begins to write all what she read and can remember. We sat quietly until she finished. Who knows when that will be? The suspense is unbearable.

# CHAPTER 11

WE HAD LUNCH, WHICH was oh so good. Lee is still frightened. She tries to play it off because the moms are starting to notice.

"So, gurls, what do you all have planned for the rest of the day? Mrs. Leng asked.

"We just staying to chill out. We might head to the skate park," Joz says as she places the last bit of ham-swiss-bacon sandwich into her mouth.

"That sounds exciting," Mrs. Leng says.

"What are you mas going to get into today? Tell more funny, embarrassing stories?" I chuckle and sip my soda.

"So you heard that?" Mrs. Fisher sips her coffee.

My cheeks turn a blush red, and I start to sweat. "Just a little." I put my fingers up to show her.

She starts to laugh, and the others join in. "It's okay, Carmella. I'm pretty sure you gurls will do the same when you get older. How do you young people say it, 'chop it up'?" Mrs. Fisher smile.

We all burst out laughing, which is great because it seems like Lee is coming back to herself.

But Joz was persistent. Lee looks and says, "I'm thinking about just burning it. I don't want no one to know what Mo'Lynn had down in her journal."

"You can burn it afterward." Joz snatched the notepad. Her eyes get big as the morning sun. She drops it, and as she looks up, a tear rolls down her cheek. "Yeah, I say we burn it." She was shaking.

"Okay, wait a minute. What in the world is going on?" I pick up the journal and start reading it. I can't put it down. I keep reading and reading and reading. All I can think about is what are we going to do with Mo'. She really needs help, like for real. Do we get the youth advisors involved? Like what do we do?

"I tell ya one thang. Burning it we will not do. Are you sure this is what you seen in the journal?"

I look over at Lee as she says, "I want to try to forget." Lee starts to pace back and forth.

"What if something can happen to us just by reading what Lee wrote by what she saw?" Joz says with her fingers in her mouth.

"I'm going to tell my mom," Lee whines a bit.

Joz stands in front of the door to stop her, then puts her hand on her shoulders, looks her in the eyes, and asked her that if we do, then what will her mom think. Joz told Lee that she thought we was supposed to handle Mo'Lynn on our own. She turns her around, walks behind her, and they sit on the edge of the bed with me.

I say with both fear and confidence, "We must make a pact that no matter what, we will get to the bottom of this. We got to know what to do. All the learning and training we have been getting from youth group, being summer-camp advisors, we must think what our leaders would do if they see this."

"Do you always have to be the voice of reason?" Lee states as she plumps the rest of her body on the bed, her hands in the air, as if she is on a roller-coaster ride. I give her the look like *You already know.*

"Ms. Reporter," Lee says as she looks at the ceiling, "you need to use your skills and get to the bottom of this."

"Why me?" Joz moans, pointing at her chest.

"Why not you?" Lee lifts up and rests her head on her hands. "This is what will make you a great reporter. You need to start now."

"You have always been so encouraging," Joz says sarcastically.

"No, I'm serious." Lee squats up in Indian style. "Reporting is what you want to do, and a great reporter is who you shall be."

"Thanks Lee." Joz and Lee smile at each other.

I look back at them both and say, "Together we can accomplish anything. Let's put our heads together and figure this thing out. Lee, can you please give me a mani-pedi 'cause these hands chil'." I look down at my nails.

"Most def 'cause I meant to tell you that last night. You know I got you." Lee smirks as she starts to work on my manicure. She always comes prepared.

Joz is brainstorming and talking so fast with excitement we have to slow her down. In the midst of the laughing, brainstorming, and pushing Joz forward to get to writing her thoughts down, I think to myself I really have great friends. We are always there for one another. We are truly a sistahood. I might add, we are all the only child in our families. I am so overjoyed that Joz came up with the sleepover, even though Má, Mrs. Leng and I did all the work. Or was it just me? I laugh to myself.

Youth group rolls around, and we are all getting into the singing and dancing. We all have a seat. Mind you, Mo' is seating right in front of me but a seat over. The youth pastor is speaking, and we are all clapping. I look down at Mo', and she is slumped down in the chair, with the back of her head hanging on the chair's back, only clapping her fingertips. One of the youth advisors bends down beside her and whispers something to her. She jumps up, fix the back of her hair, and gets up and go. I'm thinking to myself she barely has enough strength to clap, but she has enough to fix her hair, grab her bag, and go. She is so full of it. I'm trying not to judge, but I'm calling it like I see it.

I look down to my right, and Lee gives me that look like *Yelper I seen that mess too*. It's nice that Lee has come to terms with Ty and me because he was seating right next to me on my left. I look around to try to find Joz, but I don't see her anywhere. We all have a seat and begin to listen, take notes, so that we can apply to our lives what's about to be brought.

Joz has snuck out behind Mo' to see what she is up too. She followed Mo' and Rhonda to the open community area, where they sit and chat. Joz stands behind the thick plank pole, where they can't see her, but she has her phone on record so that she can get everything that's being said.

"I wanted to talk with you about the incident in the bathroom at the heaven-and-hell party. What happen?"

"I was minding my own buziness when those nosy gurls came in and messed it up."

"What did they mess up?" Rhonda looks as if *What was you really doing?*

"I really don't want to talk about it." Mo' folds her arms.

"We are going to talk about it because it's a very important matter. I understand how you feel. You must know how serious this is." Rhonda leans in a little closer to Mo'.

"Not really because I wasn't doing anything." Mo arms are still folded.

"Something happen Mo'Lynn because you passed out in the bathroom. If there is something going on, you know that you can trust me." The advisor pats her knee.

"All you do is try to get people when they are vulnerable try to get them to trust you, then when they do, you run back and gossip about it." Mo' leans back in the chair.

"I don't know to what are whom you have been dealing with in your past, but I can assure you that I'm—we are not like that here." Rhonda was still in the same position.

"What makes you so sure?" Mo asked.

"Because I know me and what you share will stay right here between us. If I need help with what you tell me, then I will ask you, can I bring someone more knowledgeable in the convo."

Meanwhile Joz is recording like no one's buziness.

"Are you upset because Mz. Cy'Queita is gone?"

"What? She is gone? Dang, I have been wondering where she went. Well, that's another person that I could trust but left without saying anything." Mo' stomps her foot.

"Mo'Lynn, people leave. That's a part of life, but there is always someone that comes along that can give you the help and guidance that you can trust."

"I guess that's you, huh?" Mo' still sounds unconvinced.

"Only if you want me to be. You can trust me, Mo'Lynn. I'm here for you whenever you want and need," Rhonda assures Mo'.

"You really mean that it will stay between us?" Mo' released her arms.

"Yes. As long as you are not causing harm to yourself are others must certainly." Rhonda stands up to leave.

"I was in the bathroom working on a potion that was perfect for that night. I started it at the Halloween party at the school, but those nosey heffas blocked it again." Mo' starts in on her story.

"Wait, what nosey heffas? Wait, what potion and why again?" Rhonda looks all confused as she sits back down.

"When I would talk with Mz. Cy'Queita, I was beginning to tell her about my potions and that I want to practice those things, and this religion crap is new to me." Mo' looks down to the side.

"Crap, huh?" Rhonda shakes her head in bewilderment.

"I didn't mean to say crap. My apologies," Mo' says sadly.

"Yes, you did, and it's what you are feeling. In due time, we will work on your choice of words. Back to the potions and why?"

"It's what I'm learning and very interested in. There are a bunch of them, and I can see how good I am if I can quit getting interrupted." Mo' sounds annoyed.

"Why do you have to do them in the place that you are choosing to?"

"Because people have to be around so I can get stronger in my power." Mo' puffs her chest up to match her words.

"So you are being dishonest?" Rhonda asked.

"How is that?" Mo' looks like she does not understand.

"Because you are trying to perform a potion and not allowing the people to consent to it." Rhonda speaks as clearly as she can.

"Why do they have too?" Mo' shrugged.

"Do you like it when people do things to you that you didn't know anything about?" The advisor leans back in her seat with her hands folded.

Joz is hiding behind the pole. She is putting the pieces together. She says to herself, *I'm going to report this right on out. Just need more I need to get more.* Before she could say more, another advisor walks up to her and ask what she is doing out of youth service. She walks really fast past the advisor and back into service.

Mo'Lynn and the other advisor look up, but all they see is the advisor who caught Joz. She walks over to them both and says, "Are you going to join us?" Before they could give an answer, everyone was coming out.

"I guess not" Mo'Lynn stands up to walk away.

Rhonda gently grabs her shoulder, hands Mo' her, card and says, "Call me so we can finish our talk." Mo' takes the card but doesn't respond.

As she walks off to head out the church, she texts the twins. HOW IS EVERYTHING GOING? RHONDA LET ME KNOW Y'ALL LEFT. PLEASE TELL MZ. CY'QUEITA I MISS HER DEARLY. THANKS, MO'LYNN. Two days later, she still hadn't gotten a text back from the twins, even though they did receive her text the same day because they had read it. Mo' could see from the text she sent them.

"Mo'Lynn texted me," Shará says.

"We don't talk to her and you better not reply," Shareé instructs.

"And why not? She can see that we read the text," Shará snaps.

"And?" Shareé snapped right back.

"Whatever. You can be so rude at times." Shará roll her eyes in annoyance.

"Uh-huh," Shareé replies without a care.

On the way to the cars, Joz grab us, and we walk off to be alone. Ty shouts, "Oh, so it's like that then?" with his hands in the air. I look over my shoulder as Joz pull's my arm and smiles at Ty as she waves him off.

"I have something you guys need to hear." Joz holds up her phone.

We began to listen, and Mr. Fisher comes by. "Girls, it's time to go."

"In a minute, Dad," Joz says in utter annoyance; she doesn't even look up.

"No, right now, young lady," Mr. Fisher says as he looks at her like *I'm not moving until you move.* Just like that.

Joz stumps her foot and screams, "Uhhhh. I will hit you guys up lata."

We say okay and head to our cars to go on our separate ways.

Before I made it home, Joz had sent out a group text to Lee and me, titled YOU CAN'T TELL ANYONE. As I began to listen to it, I hear a knock at my door. "Are you coming down? You have a visitor." I hear Má' say. I look puzzled and drop my phone on the bed and head downstairs. Surprise, but not surprised, it's Ty. He stands there with a big smile on his face.

"Hey." I reach out to hug him. As we release each other, he grabs my hand, and we sit on the big swing. I grab the blanket draped over the back.

"You cold?" Ty asks.

I raised an eyebrow and say, "Don't play." He chuckle a bit and get under the blanket. "Umm, you must be too." I look at him.

"Not really. I just want to be close to you."

I blushed.

"I have been missing you so I decided to come by so we can catch up." He's giving me that look again.

"On what?" I ask, not giving in to his look.

"Us, life, what have you been up too. How is the job?" Ty asks as he shrugs a bit.

"Wow, it has been a minute huh?" I laugh.

Ty looks me dead in my eyes. It's always like he is looking straight through me or something—straight to my soul. One day, I will ask him what he sees. Today won't be that day.

"Work is going good. I like it. Been getting closer to my saving goal for me a car. I like how you all come up there every now and then just to chill out. Also been trying to figure out Mo'."

"Why are you doing that? And can we not talk about her?" Ty is already over it you can hear it in his voice.

"She is kicking it with us now, so we need to become good friends. Oh, did I tell ya Lee and I are back buddies again?"

"You didn't have to tell me. We all can see it. I'm happy for you two."

"Other than that, nothing too much has been going on. What's been up with you?" I was thinking we really needed some hot chocolate.

"I want to make absolutely sure that you guys are coming to the cabin for Christmas and New Year's?"

As Ty is talking, I'm thinking I don't remember even saying anything to my parents about it. I will ask them today. "To be honest, I haven't asked my parents, but I will today for sure."

"Haven't asked your parents what?" Má comes out with so-hot cocoa. Ty's has marshmallows.

"If we can go to their log cabin for Christmas and New Year's." I sip this good ol' hot, hot cocoa.

"Oh, that's a done deal. Your father and I already talked it over with Sr. and Ms. Claretha." Má says as she walks away.

"But how when I forgot to ask you awhile back?" I look toward the front door.

Má answers as she stops the screen door with her hand, "Ms. Claretha mentioned it to me at the sleepover, then I told Dad about it once he got home, and then we agreed. We let them know at church today." Má walks back into the house.

"There's your answer."

"And a great answer it is." Ty toast his cocoa to mine. "We are going to have a great time. Just to let you know a few thangs. We only use the landline phone. My parents say we are up there to unwind, to spend time with each other, bond, and have connection time."

"All that, huh?" I raise both my eyebrows. I'm unsure about all this, but it seems lit. It will be a lot of fun.

"Besides there is a lot of stuff to do, and you will like it, I'm sure." Ty keeps talking even after I respond.

"At least one of us is." I push him playfully.

We both laugh and just chill out a bit. When I'm with Ty, it's is like nothing else is going on and it feels just right. I'm so happy that everything is set right with everyone involved.

As we are chillaxin' on the swing, Ty gets a text from Telion. As he reads, it he has this serious look on his face. I touch his shoulders. "Is everything okay?"

He looks up and shakes his head. "No"

"Can you tell me about it?" I look concerned.

"Not now, can't mess up the bro code." He stands up.

"You leaving?"

"I don't want to, but Telion needs me right now."

As we embrace and I watch him walk and disappear up the street, I can't help but wonder what it could have been. I grab our cups after folding the blanket and draping it back over the swing and head into the warmth of my home. I head straight for the kitchen to put the cups in the sink.

I look out the window, and Dad and Má are out back cuddled up with blankets in front of the bomb fire. As I watch them, I say to myself, "If that bomb fire could talk, what stories would it tell?" I place my hand up to the window, smiling, and head upstairs. I grab my phone off the bed and see that Joz and Lee has just been going in on Mo'. I'm not going to text back. I'm going to video chat them from my computer.

"Winner, winner, chicken dinner, where have you been?" Joz could barely even wait to see my face on the screen.

"Touch your nose," I tell her.

"You know I already did it, so spill it."

"If you must know, I was chillin' with Ty. He came by for a bit." I smile inside, but I know it is showing on the outside. "He got a text from Telion and had to leave." As I'm talking, I look at Lee to make sure she is kool, not uncomfortable or nothing. She looks as if she is not paying us any attention. She is doing something else.

"Lee, wuz up?" I say to get her attention.

"I heard you guys. I'm also trying to practice this new design is all."

"I hope I get it because I know it's going to be tight." I do a shimmy.

She looks up and smile, then she says, "Go ahead, I can hear ya."

I was thinking, *Now you two was just going in by text. Now you working on a design.* Maybe I should look at the time these texts took place and stop jumping to conclusions.

"Mo'Lynn has really done it now." Joz starts in.

"Carmella, can you come down here please?" I hear Má calling from downstairs.

"I will have to chat with yawl in a bit. Má is calling." I disconnect and head downstairs, shouting, "Here I come. Where are you?"

"I'm in the kitchen," Má shouts back.

"Hey, Má, what's going on?"

"I need you to help with baking my tasty little shortcakes."

"Really?" I say, thinking to myself, *Wasn't you just outside with Dad?*

"What, you have something betta else to do?"

"I was video chatting with the gurls about some stuff."

"Is that more important than helping me out a bit?" Má hands me a bowl.

"Naw, Má, it's kool." I take the bowl to begin putting mixer in it.

"Naw?" Má's voice goes up a bit.

"No, ma'am." I don't even look up from the bowl.

"It will only be a little while, then you can go back to chopping it up with your gurls." Má points and nod.

"Má"—I laughed—"you and your young talk."

"I'm trying to speak in a language you understand is all."

"Oh okay." I give Má that mature smile. Even though I don't ever say it, I love cooking in the kitchen with Má, tasting her creative treats, watching her do her thang. It just amazes me. As we finish up about fifty of the tasty little shortcakes, there is a knock at the door.

"I will get it." I get up from the stool and head to the door, open it, and its Mrs. Fisher.

"Hello, Carmella, how are you?"

"Good. Má is in the kitchen." As Mrs. Fisher heads to the kitchen, I yell and say, "I'm going back up to my room, Má."

"Okay, sweet love!" Má yells back.

"What do you have going on today?" Mrs. Fisher asked as she placed her purse on the chair next to the one I was sitting down in.

"I have to get this order out. You want something to drink?"

"I can get it myself. I have been here enough times. I know where everything is." Mrs. Fisher gets up to help herself.

"What brings you my way and without calling first?" Má gives Mrs. Fisher that look like *You know it's all good.*

"There is something going on, and I just need some advice." She takes a seat on the stool.

"Okay, shoot." Má says, still mixing.

"At practice last night, the leaders wanted to be there all night— well, okay not all night. We left at about 9:00 p.m."

"Okay, what's the problem?" Má starts to put the batter in the baking pan.

"We shouldn't be at practice that late." Mrs. Fisher is a little upset.

"Have you addressed it to the Leader?"

"Yes, but there is always an attitude. And it's not just me, it's other members too."

"Maybe the group should have a pow-wow session. Not to tear anyone down, just to voice your concern's and have solutions to the problem. Then pray on it together before and after." Má places the baking pans in the oven.

"What if it doesn't work?" Mrs. Fisher was eating leftover batter out of the bowl.

"And what if it does?" Má wipes her hands on her apron. "It doesn't hurt to try, I tell ya that. Now tell me what's all these cakes for and can I taste one?"

"No, ma'am, you can't have one. I baked just enough for this order. I have to deliver them today." Má starts to wipe the counters down.

"So proud of you," Ms. Fisher says. "You keep moving forward no matter what."

"I have too. Nothing else to do but what I know to do. If I don't, I would probably go insane. Quick question?"

"Wuz up?" Mrs. Fisher put the empty bowl in the sink.

Má leans in to whisper as if someone else is in the kitchen with them. "Do you know what the girls got going on? They have been a little secretly weird since the sleepover?"

"Which girls are you referring too, and why are we whispering?" Mrs. Fisher leans in, mocking Má.

"Our girls!" Má slaps the counter.

"No. Why Carmella say something?" Mrs. Fisher gives that look like *You know I will be on Joz's butt.*

"No, but she is on her phone more than normal is all." Má looks bothered a bit.

"I say let's just wait it out. If they need us, they will come to us." Mrs. Fisher was still thinking of them little cakes.

"You are so right about that." Má nods.

"Let me help place them in the boxes, and I will help you deliver them." Mrs. Fisher gets to helping.

"Thanks. I need the help. Let me run upstairs to get you a logo shirt to put on, then we can load the Jeep." As Má comes upstairs she opens my door and says, "I'm about to deliver my little cakes. I will be right back."

"Okay." I look up at Má to let her know I heard her. She shuts the door. The whole time I'm thinking, *I hope she didn't hear us.*

"She didn't hear us, did she?" Joz says.

"I was just thinking that," I told both of them. "You really need to stay out my head, Joz."

We all laugh.

"Here is your shirt. You can change in the bathroom, then help me finish loading the Jeep." Má hands Mrs. Fisher the shirt.

"Okay, I will meet you at the Jeep." Mrs. Fisher heads to change into the shirt.

Má begins to load the car, and Mrs. Fisher joins in. They buckle in, and off they go to their destination.

"Are you going to tell me where we are going?" Mrs. Fisher is putting on lipstick, using the car mirror.

"You will see. We are about to pull up." Má smiles.

Mrs. Fisher slaps Má's shoulder. "Are you serious? Don't play. This is where your delivery is? This is one of the best bistros in town. Wow, I'm excited to be your friend." Mrs. Fisher screams like a schoolgirl crushing on her first crush.

"You are something else. Come on, let's get these cakes in." Má puts the car in park and unbuckle her seatbelt. The chef meets them at the door. She tells Má that it's such a pleasure to have her little cakes at the bistro, hoping one day they can be added to the menu. Má says, "Just let me know 'cause I'm ready."

As they drive away, Mrs. Fisher is still in awe. "Baś, do you know—she says as she looks at Má—"what that bistro really is?"

"Yes, I do," Má says humbly. "Actually, the chef sought me out."

"Are you serious?" Mrs. Fisher eyes are wide open, saying tell me more.

"Yes. She said she was at a party, and she tasted my food, desserts, and drinks. She knew she had to get my creations at Baśh the bistro."

"You are so in the door." You can hear the pride in Mrs. Fisher's voice.

"I always tell myself no job is too small. There is always a lesson in it. No matter what I always do my best 'cause that's my name out there."

"Well, you have done it this time, and I'm so happy I got to share it with ya," Mrs. Fisher says.

I can see them pull up on the driveway. "So how did it go?" I lean on the porch as they are heading inside.

"Your mom didn't tell me where we were going, but when she showed me—umm, I'm still in awe." Mrs. Fisher is hugging herself with her eyes close, as if she is going there again in her memories.

"Yeah, Má does that," I say with my arms folded. Má touches me on the head as they walk up the steps and head in the house.

"Wait, that sounds like my mom," Joz says.

"It was. I thought I told you she was here."

"Man, she left and didn't tell me where she was going. That's messed up. I could be over there too," Joz whines. "I'm about to text her right now."

Joz is texting her mother. We all are still on video chat, trying to make a resolution of what we are going to do about Mo'.

"How about we just leave the gurl alone? Let her do her, and if it involves us, we will handle it, then if not, then not, and we keep moving," Lee says with no energy in her voice.

"Naw! Naw! Naw! Naw!" Joz speaks up quickly. "She has been doing too much, and it's time for her to get dealt with."

"Okay, Miss Fired Up, what do you have in mind?" Lee gives her that look like *You aint gone do nothing. You just all talk.*

"Don't know…that's why I need help." Joz gives a blank look.

"When you know what you need help with, then you let us know. I have to go." Lee disconnected the from the chat.

I tell Joz that we will come up with something, but for now let's let it rest. She says, "No I will keep thinking because I'm going to get her. We are going to get her."

"Peace. Out." I disconnect the chat from Joz. She can be very nerve-racking at times. I just chill out on the porch for a bit. It's starts to get too cold for me, so I head back in the house.

# CHAPTER 12

As I WALK BACK into the house, I hear Má and Mrs. Fisher cackling about something, so I decide to chill on the couch. I send Ty a text just to see what has been going on. I also send the twins a text. I really miss them—well, one more than the other. I laugh to myself. Haven't really talked to Teli, but I have seen him around. Just when I was about to go into another thought, I feel a kiss on the top of my head and hear a voice say, "Hey, sweetheart, how was your day?" I look up—it's Dad.

"I should be asking you that. Do you want me to get you something to drink? A snack are something?" I ask as Dad sits in his chair.

"That would be nice."

I go in the kitchen, grab Dad's request, and Má looks and says, "I heard your dad. He back home?"

"Yes, ma'am." I pour Dad's juice with a little bounce.

Mrs. Fisher gets her things and says as she heads for the door, "I will chat with ya lata." She also says bye to Dad as she leaves.

I come back in the living room with Dad's snacks and drinks. To be honest, it's one of his smooviees he likes. He throws his head up a bit, then leans back in his chair with his eyes closed. I hand Dad his smooviee, didn't know Má was right behind me. She grabs ahold of Dad's hand and kiss him softly on the lips. Dad smiles, not even opening his eyes. I watch my parents in awe 'cause no matter what life throws at them, they still sincerely love each other and, most times, act like they are the only two in the world.

"Well, I will let you be alone." I turn to go toward the stairs.

"No, Carmella, have a seat. We need to discuss something with you."

It sounds serious so I sit on the couch. Dad pops his chair up right with his elbows to his knees, places his hands in a prayer position, rests his cheeks on his hands. Má is sitting on the arm of the chair, with an arm around his shoulder and another on his chest. She looks at Dad and says, "Go on, bae, tell her."

Dad breathes deeply and sighs. "We are prego."

I look confused. "Like the sauce?"

"What? Chil, naw. You are having a little brother are sister."

"That's kool." I nod.

"Really? That's all you have to say?" Dad asked.

"Yeah. I mean, yes. I will be a big sista. Sounds great to me." I head upstairs with not a care in the world.

"That went well." Má looks at Dad.

"Why would you think it wouldn't? We have raised a mature young lady. I knew she would be cool with it. That's my gurl," Dad assures Má, then leans back into his chair and close his eyes again.

"You mean our gurl," Má says as she slides in Dad's chair with him.

"Yes, our gurl," Dad says. They both just sigh in agreement.

Back into the swing of thangs. While at work, the whole crew comes in at my lunch time. I warn them ahead of time that my lunch is only thirty minutes. They all laugh. I really miss the twins, so I call them—no answer.

"Why must you keep calling them? They don't even answer, and how you know that's still their number?" Joz puts a fry in her mouth.

"I don't know," I say as I snatch a fry out of her hand. "I just miss them and want to let them know." She lifted up her left brow as an *Okay, yeah right.*

"It's good to see you, Telion." Lee changes the subject. He smiles, but she doesn't stop there. "Soo what have you been up to?"

"A little this and that," he replies as he takes a bite of his burger and look over at Ty. Ty does this *Wuz up.*

"I see. I see you don't want to talk about it. Its kool." Lee winks.

"Naw, it's just there is nothing to talk about," Telion says as he sips his soda.

So we all just start to talk about this and that. I let them know my lunch break is over, but as I get up, Mo' walks in.

"Well, well, well, look who decides to walk in?" Joz stands up to act like she is letting me out.

"What are you talking about?" Mo' walks right by her to the counter to place her order.

"You didn't get the message that we all were chillin' here today?" Joz sits back down.

"Nope." Mo' doesn't even turn from the counter.

"Okay, I see how its is."

Once Mo' gets her order, she goes to sit at a whole different table. The looks that Joz is giving her is like she is slicing her open with her thoughts. I watch closely as I'm at the register, taking customers one by one.

I see that things are just not going to get right at all with those two. There must be a way we can make this right. As everyone is leaving, Mo' is still sitting alone. I don't remember how long she has been there. I walk over to her and let her know that we are about to close and she is the only one left. She looks up at me with this face I have never seen anyone have.

"Are you okay?" I ask as I clean her things from the table.

She just looks at me like she can't hear anything I just said. I go get the manager to help because my manager tonight is also one of the youth advisors. By the time I went to get her and came back, Mo' was gone. I explain to her what I have seen, so we pray together and lock up. Má is waiting outside in the car. I wave to my manager, then we all get in our cars.

As Má begins to drive off, I ask, "When can I take my driver's test?"

"You know when—on your sixteenth birthday. You really think you ready?" Má take a quick look at me then back to her driving.

"Yes, I am, but since that is like a year away, I can be practicing."

"You are so right. We can get that started for ya. I will have a talk with your dad and see what we can do about that."

I just nodded. On the ride home, I'm excited because I will be learning to drive, then I can get my license and then get my car.

Meanwhile back at my place of work, the manager and I didn't notice that Mo' was still there. She hid in the bathroom, and once all the doors were locked, lights out, and the alarm was on, she came out. Little did she know that there were cameras inside the fast-food joint. Good ones too that you can even see whomever in the dark. None in the bathroom, though—that is illegal, I think. It should be 'cause that's privacy right there.

I get the text from my manager to come in at regular shift because she has to talk to me. I didn't see anything happening; it was just a regular Saturday morning. As Má drops me off, we see cops and the manager inside. Má says, "Oh, I'm not leaving you here until I know it's safe." She walks in with me, and right away I can see this disgust, disbelief, and disappointment on her face.

"Hey, manager, what is going on?" I touch her shoulder. She told me to have a seat; there was something she needed to show me. So of course, I did. The cop is there taking notes, writing things down and watching our every move.

The manager hands me the video, and as I watch, I already know who it is. I look up at my manager and is like, *Really! You got to be kidding*. She sits across from me, where Má is, and touching my hand, she says, "I just wanted to see if you see what I seen on the video."

In my head, I'm like, *Is she QRZ are what?* She was in the video going through the, well, trying to get in, the cash register. Then she went to the safe. She couldn't get in, so she started trying to cook herself something but doesn't know how to work the equipment. I give Má and the manager a concerned look because I don't want to tell on her. I really think she needs some serious help.

My parents raised me to tell the truth at all times. I didn't have to say anything. The manager told the cops who it was and everything she knew about Mo'. All I could think of was if she had a cell phone that I could contact her on. I could give her a heads up and ask her why she would do such a thing. I am laughing a bit inside at her, like *Why?* Once the cop leaves with the manager's statement, Má gives me that look like I'm safe so she is leaving also and that she is going to contact Mo's grandmother. Má didn't even make it to the car good. I could see her already on the phone. Mo' really didn't do too much damage really. She dirtied up one burner trying to make a meat patty, but that was it. When she left, she left the back door wide open. Her fingerprints were everywhere and on everything she touched. I still feel bad for her because there must be a reason why she is acting out like this. I'm going to keep this to myself for now because for some reason, I care about this gurl. She is okay, I guess—well, was—until she started acting weird and doing no nonsense stuff.

I look out the window, I see Má put her phone down and drive off; she wasn't on the phone long, must have left a message. "Mrs. Racheal, I need you to call me. It's very important. It concerns Mo'Lynn. Please get back to me as soon as you can. Thank you." Probably sounded something like that. LOL.

Work shift is over, and as I go to the car, Má is in the passenger seat. I had the biggest smile on my face as I got into the driver's seat. Má winks at me, and we do a few rounds in the parking lot, parking, parallel parking, going through cones and stuff.

As I place the car in park, Má says, "What are you doing?"

"I'm going to clean the parking lot, so then you can drive us home," I say as I open the car door. I put everything neatly in the trunk 'cause if I don't, Dad will have a fit. I look through the back windshield, and Má is still sitting in the passenger seat. I get in on the driver's side.

"What you are doing?" I asked, one of my legs still hanging out the car door.

"Since you are working towards getting your permit, then now is a better time as any. You will be driving yourself to work and back home with me in the car, of course. Your father and I have already added you to the insurance. Now let's get this show on the road. Take your time, and let's see what you got." Má looks like *Come on naw.*

I look at her all surprised, but I also tell myself I can't freeze up now. No way. First permit, then driver's license, then car. Let's show Má what all the studying and the fake driving I have been doing in my room with the fake car at the foot of my bed has taught me. Okay, yeah, I will get to that later. My hands are at ten and two. I began to pull off into the street, but first I put my blinker on, showing I was turning left. I look to make sure that it's safe to pull out, then heading home we go. I make sure that I ease on the break as I pull up to the red lights. I also slow down briefly at the yellow light to prepare myself to stop if it turns red. I have been watching my parents at it. When I was younger, they used to let me sit on their lap and drive when we were in the country or in a big, empty parking lot. I got the feel of the steering wheel that way. Before I knew it, I was parking in the driveway. I place the car in park, looked over at Má. She didn't say a word, just gave me that smile to let me know I did good. She had been texting on her phone the whole ride or acting like she was.

I get out with the keys in hand, push the auto lock, and proceed to the house. Má is now on the phone, talking I don't know to whom, so I place the key in the door, and we head into the house. I put the keys in the front bowl by the door and head up to my room.

I began to clean my fake car I made with two pillows and an old steering wheel cover that I placed on a cardboard box and hooked it up a bit. As I finish cleaning it up, I say to myself I don't need it anymore. I get my journal and write everything about today and me driving. I felt so grown up just without all the responsibility. For Má to say that from now on, I will be driving myself to work and back home, oh yeah. I'm going to see if I can get more workdays. LOL. I head downstairs, and Má is still on the phone, but this time it's on speaker, and I recognize the voice—it's Mrs. Racheal, Mo's grandmother. They are talking about Mo', so yes, I'm eavesdropping. I stand in the corner right where I can't be seen from the kitchen. I can see when Dad will come in the front door, and I can hear the convo so clearly.

They are both going on and on. It's getting really juicy. Mrs. Racheal tells Má about Mo's counseling session and how they were going really good, but now that Mz. Cy'Queita has left, they are looking for someone new. I was hoping they would get into why Mz. Cy'Queita and the twins left, but they never did. Má began to keep Mrs. Racheal encouraged and let her know that if she likes, Mo' can come and be with me sometimes.

I must have gotten so wrapped up in my own thoughts and what was said that the next thing I hear was, "Since when do we eavesdrop, lady?" Dad touches my shoulder.

"My apologies, I just really wanted to hear about Mo', no disrespect." I give Dad the sad eyes, but it doesn't work.

"I'm not the one you have to apologize too."

As we both walk into the kitchen, Má is still fully engaged in her convo with Mrs. Racheal she didn't even notice us standing there. Má has made some good-looking chicken salad with three different homemade dressing. I give Dad the looks, and he looks back at me to gesture to Má that we are standing here. I don't. He goes over and kisses Má on the cheek. She looks up, smiles, says hello, and let Mrs. Racheal know they can catch up tomorrow as she has to place dinner on the table and thangs. They both say bye.

"Má, this salad is so good," I say as I'm smacking.

"Don't you have something to tell your mother?" Dad messed that compliment right on up.

"Tell me what?" Má places food in her mouth.

"Like how much you loved the drive home?" I'm trying to change the subject.

"No." Má gave me a QRZ look. "What you mean chil?"

"I liked the drive home." With a sad voice, I go ahead and let Má know what's going on. "Dad caught me eavesdropping on the convo with you and Mrs. Racheal. I want to say that I apologize and it want ever happen again. I know we don't snoop are eavesdrop on private convos with each other. We respect each other's privacy."

"You dog on right, young lady. Now are you apologizing because you got caught are because you really mean it." Má points her folk at me.

"At first it was because I got caught, but now that I see where I went wrong, it is both." I look at Má with recognized eyes.

"Good girl," Má says as she keeps eating.

Then Dad chimes in with excitement. "So how was the drive home?"

I look over at Dad like he just was not here when we had the last convo, but I engage him anyhow. "I loved the drive, Dad. I'm thinking about asking for more days to work so I can get more driving practice in." I do my happy dance and take a bite of salad.

They both laugh, and Dad looks over, "Don't get too ahead of yourself. You still have other things on your plate. One step at a time."

I nod in agreement. Dad and I cleaned off the table after dinner, then we all chilled out in front of the TV, watching a good old mystery-detective show.

# CHAPTER 13

SCHOOL, YOU'RE BACK AGAIN, but too soon for Thanksgiving break. I had still been thinking about Mo' and what she had done. I have been seeing her around at school, but she is living her best life because she goes around as if nothing has happened. I also still see her at youth group. Joz is still trying to pay Mo' back for all she has done to her, but she still hasn't done anything yet. Like I told her, she should just let it go—but no, Joz and her grudges.

My lunch time rolls around, and we all are at our booth. I think to myself that now maybe is the time to pull Mo' to the side to see where her headspace is. I walk to once I see her almost done with her food. "Hey, Mo', can I talk to you for a sec?"

"Sure, why not," she says as she gets up, and we walk over to the gate right before leaving the lunch area outside.

"You okay?"

"Yeah. Why you ask that?" She looks at me confused.

"Well, you have been acting strange and just doing whatsoever without a care." I'm still looking concerned.

"You talking about what I think you are talking about?"

"Yeah." I give her that look like she doesn't know.

"It's none of your buziness, to be honest. You need to learn to just stay out my buziness." She smarts with a pout and folded arms.

I'm saying to myself, *Don't do it, C. Don't do it.* "You are always offensive. I'm just asking you a question and trying to help you out." I realized by this point I'm getting loud because we have some people staring.

"Like I said," she says as she rolls her eyes and begin to walk off.

Out of nowhere, Joz puts her hand right on Mo's shoulder and whispers in her ear, but loud enough so I could hear. "You want get away with any of it!"

Mo' slaps her hand away, goes back to the table, gets her belongings, places her tray in the tray holder, and walks out.

I just stand there looking at Joz. She says to me in a manner like when I saw her mother talking to her through her teeth, "I told you to stop concerning yourself!" She grabs my shoulder and heads me back to the booth.

All eyes are on us. Lee is just shaking her head as she does what she does. Ty places his arm around my shoulders to let me know without saying a word that he is here for me, and Teli doesn't know nothing going on because he has his earphones on and he is dribbling that basketball. We put out trays up and head to our class. I'm thinking to myself, *Oh she will not be coming to no house kicking it with me. No time. Period. I'm going to let Má know too. Mo' wants to be done, then we are done.*

On the bus ride home, I'm not saying much at all, but Ty and Lee are having a good time. The bus reaches our stop. Ty always gets off with me then walks half a block home. As we get off the bus, I tell Ty, "Hey, I'm going to walk you home today."

He smiles. "Are you sure?"

"Yeah, why not? You always walking me home. I will walk you today." I shrugged.

He replies with, "Today, huh?"

We laugh, and I walk Ty to his door, hug him, and walk the half-block back to my house. I must have been in such deep thought that I didn't notice Ty following me until his phone rang. I look back, and he, looking all nervous, answers his phone, waves at me, turns quickly, and heads home. I just laugh and smile on the inside 'cause it's very nice how he makes sure that I'm all right.

I head into the house. Má is in the kitchen, baking something that I can taste just by smelling it. Her belly hasn't gotten bigger. I do remember them telling me that she was prego.

"So how was school?" Má asked.

"Do you really want to know?" I say. *I want to tell you, but then again, I don't because I don't really want to hear what you will say*, I say to myself. "At lunch today, I tried to talk to Mo', just to see where her headspace was and what's up with her. She gets all defensive and starts to go off and tell me to mind my buziness and stop being nosey cause she is not going to tell me anything."

Má gives me a blank stare, so I keep going on. "Since that's how she feel, then we want be hanging out 'cause I was really concerned about her, but hey, it is what it is," I say, a little hurt and aggravated at this point.

"Well, maybe you two can just start over."

"Naw, Má, I don't want to do that. I don't want to have nothing to do with her. I will just leave her alone as she wishes."

"Okay then, I will let Mrs. Racheal know that the offer has been withdrawn, and you and Mo'Lynn will not be hanging out." Má sounds disappointed.

I get up from the stool, hug Má because she has a big heart and she loves to help anyway she can—that's where I get it from, I understand. I ask if I can try the new recipe she is creating when she is done. She looks up with the grown-people smirk and says, "You are going to love it. I'm trying new thangs for Thanksgiving," as she does a one-shoulder shimmy. "I will still invite Mrs. Racheal and her family over so get it together."

"It's kool with me, Má. Your cooking always brings out the best in er'body." I grab an apple and head to the front porch. I have no homework and don't have to go to work, so I guess I will chill on the porch in the cold. It's a nice, breezy cold, but not too cold. I thought I would until my phone buzzed with a text from Joz, saying, I HAVE FOUND A WAY TO CATCH MO'LYNN IN WHATEVER ACT SHE IS DOING AT THE TIME. I WILL JUST HAVE MY RECORDER ON, AND VIDEO CAUSE WE ARE GOING TO CATCH HER.

THAT SOUNDS LIKE A LOT, Lee chimes in.

YEAH, I agree as we keep texting back and forth.

Joz informs us that we won't be doing anything but just be there, she will handle the rest, and all we have to do is get together.

MÁ IS SENDING OUT INVITATION FOR THANKSGIVING.

Joz texted back, OK WE WILL WAIT TILL EVERYONE AGREE TO COME. SO THAT MEANS IT'S ALL HAPPENING AT YOUR HOUSE WHERE IT ALL STARTED IN THE 1ST PLACE.

WHATEVER, I text with my tongue out.

Lee texted back, T2YL.

I just chill on the porch on the swing, enjoying the nice breeze with my electric blanket and journal.

Má sent out a mass text to everyone, then she did a follow-up call once we got closer to Thanksgiving. Mind you, it's two weeks away, but Má has been preparing food and deserts since the first of the month. She has always been very organized and runs everything with excellence. As she is preparing for Thanksgiving, she still has orders coming in that she is fulfilling and delivering. So yes, that means Mrs. Fisher comes over and helps out a lot.

The menu for Thanksgiving has not been set in stone yet because all the families get to bring a dish from their culture. We have Thanksgiving from all over the world right in our home. We also have to get the games ready. We have a new family coming this year—Mo' and her grandparents. Má also has everyone bring extra food, and she cooks a lot just in case we come across a family in need and don't have anywhere to go. They are always welcome to come to our house. We take food down to the shelter and serve breakfast there on Thanksgiving. Má came up with that idea because she said why have them wait 'til dinner. They get a really good, hearty breakfast. Maybe someday someone will give them lunch. Hey, I can present that to Rhonda and see if that's something we youth can do. If I do that, then I will need to really good menu prepared. It's a really good idea. I will bring it up to Má and get her input and see what we can do. I can also see on Thanksgiving what everyone thinks when they come over. If everything goes well, then next year, at the shelter, there will be served breakfast, lunch, and dinner. I do a little dance. *Yeah, I got this! I got this.*

Seems like everyone is showing up. I hope to keep the drama down between Joz and Mo'. I still haven't come up with any games. It needs to be something we all can play, get the dads from watching that game. Now that's going to be very hard to do. Maybe we can play games after the football game goes off—don't want to get my head bitten off. We need games everyone can play together; that's the whole point of Thanksgiving, right? Friendsgiving, whatever you want to call it. Everyone will be coming except Mz. Cy'Queita and the twins. I'm going to talk to Má to see if she talked to them about coming. I hope she sent an invite. I know the twins said they won't be coming back, but I miss them shut.

As it is getting closer to Thanksgiving day, I ask Má while she is baking up something good. "Good morning, Má! Did you send an invite out to Mz. Cy'Queita and the twins?"

"Have you read my mind are something." Má keeps watching the oven. "I know you wasn't near me when I sent the invite."

At this moment, I smile but still waited with anticipation for my answer.

"Cy'Quieta called me back and let me know that she thanks me for the invite, but they will not be coming this time."

As my face drops in sadness, I hear Mrs. Fisher voice. "Who want be coming and where?" she asks with certainty.

"Cy'Quieta and the twins want be coming for Thanksgiving." Má takes the baked goods out the oven.

"Aww, that's too bad. We really need to find out what happen." Mrs. Fisher takes a seat.

I let them know that I will be going outside. As I open the front door, to my surprise, Ty is walking up to the house.

"Why the long face, C?" he says as he walks up and helps me take the blanket from the back of the swing and have a seat.

"The twins want be coming for Thanksgiving," I say sadly.

"Okay," Ty says with no emotion at all.

I gave him the *Really?* look. You can see that he understands the look because the he tries to drum up something to say. As he opens his mouth to say whatever, I stop him and say, "Never mind. I get it." He smiles as we chillax on the porch swing with the warm blanket. He is talking about food, like always, and he brought up Christmas, something about New Year's, but I'm really not paying any attention because all I can think about is how Mz. Cy'Queita and the twins not coming and how I see that they are reading my text and not replying back. *Ughhhh!*

Ty gets a call and has to leave. I head back into the house and talk to Má about Thanksgiving lunch next year. She asked, "Why we can't do it this year?"

"Because Thanksgiving is two weeks away, and I don't know how many teens we will have."

She goes to say, "Sounds like an excuse, but I know you like to have a definite plan."

"I do, and I haven't brought it up to the advisors yet."

"You right, sweetheart. Order is key."

Má keeps working to fulfill her order. I head upstairs to my room with so much on my mind I plop on the bed and decide to send out a group text and see what suggestions everyone can come up with about the games we should play. I love making memories, having traditions being together you know. As I waited for replies, I didn't notice until I woke up from my sleep that I had taken a nap. Thinking takes a lot of energy, good energy maybe. LOL.

The next thang I knew, Hello, Thanksgiving.

# CHAPTER 14

THE MORNING OF THANKSGIVING, we are heading to the shelter to serve breakfast. Once we arrive, some of the youth advisors are there also, so I typed up my idea all nice and everything and gave it to each of them. I let them know what my ideas were and that I did the research and Má helped me with the budget and food menu. One of them let me know that they will get it to the youth pastor because he has the final say and that this is a great idea that needs to be acted upon. I told her thank you, and then we began to set up the breakfast Má and some others prepared.

We treat the less fortunate like royalty. I don't like to call them homeless 'cause to be honest, people can stay in nice homes but are still homeless. Homelessness is a state of mind, and society thinks that if you don't have an apartment, house are whatever than you are homeless in my mind not so true. Home is where your heart is and what you make of it. I call them "less fortunate" because maybe at this time they are just a little down and need a pick-me-up. Life has thrown them a curveball, and until they can adjust, they need a little help, as we all do at times someway, somehow. Now let's talk about this spread because I'm telling you, I will be on this soapbox for a minute.

The spread is laid out on a long table. Adults are in the kitchen preparing. The youth are out serving, and we both are cleaning and keeping things in order as we go. We are working as a well-oiled machine in togetherness and love.

We have pancakes, waffles, eggs, omelets, which come with many choices of fruit, coffee, juice (100 percent—Má doesn't play), water, and tea. We have bacon, turkey, and pork, and we even have a vegan selection. We have four different kinds of sausages. When Má does her thang, she goes all out to truly cater to everyone's taste or palate. We have some coming up to the serving line, and others are being served due to them not being able to come to the line. We have a kid's area set up, so after they eat, they can chill out while the parents talk 'cause you know they can talk. LOL. Breakfast is from 6:00 a.m. to 10:00 a.m. Every year, we always serve everyone then send them with to-go plates. Once everyone is fully fed and has gone with their plates, we begin the cleanup, and then we all head home to get ready for whatever we have planned for Thanksgiving. As we make it home, it smells so good through the door. It had me thinking I forgot to tell ya we had yogurt and homemade parfaits at the breakfast.

There is only a short time to take a breather because everyone will start to come over at about 5:00 p.m. because we will eat at 6:00 p.m. Don't know why to this day it takes so long for us to eat. I was ready to chow down.

Everyone has made their way to the house, and we have dishes from every culture—I love it. We might not be able to go visit some of the places, but we have food from there, so we still get the experience in a way. We have Creole, Hawaiian, Asian, Southern, and some new dishes that others wanted to try cooking. I hope they practiced before they brought the concoction over here for others to try. We had desserts of all kinds.

After grace, we all eat, then the men take their dessert and go watch the game. Then come the dominoes, then family games. That's how things go on this day. We are all spread throughout the house—kitchen, living room, dining area—pretty much doing our own thing. Still together, I guess, 'cause we are all in the house. The sounds of laughter, togetherness, fun, and love, it's the greatest sounds of feelings. Man, I love the holidays. As I'm basking in the atmosphere, trying to take it all in, I look over at Joz, and to my surprise, her and Mo' are getting along. Joz, Mo', Teli, and Ty are playing Monopoly: The Cards. It is getting heated, but in a good way.

Maybe this will show us another side of Mo', and she can see sides of us. Lee is drawing, as she always does. As she continues, the heat going on in the Monopoly game. I look over and take a peek at her drawing, which is really good by the way. Mo' wins that hand, then we all get in the game and play. We go from card games to board games. Má and the ladies are playing spades and pinochle. I don't want this day to end. We are out of school until Tuesday of next week. We have time to just chill on this day until then. I know I'm a serious dreamer.

Nighttime rolls around, and as cold as it is outside, still no snow, we all go to the firepit with warm blankets and hot cocoa (no marshmallows in mine) and tea. We talk about everything and nothing, most importantly what we are thankful for. You can see everyone is having a great time until Mo' goes off on a tangent. We all look at her like she is QRZ.

Her grandfather doesn't pull her to the side, like her grandmother has done before. He deals with her biscuits right there. "Mo'Lynn, what is the problem? What is going on with you right in this moment?" He says it so calmly Mo' squirms down in her chair and puts her head down. He doesn't accept that, though. "No, sit up and tells us what is going on." This time, his voice is still stern but calm.

She looks up and say, "I'm not used to this, all this happiness, and I know it's not going to last, so I got to always be prepared no matter what."

"It doesn't last because you choose to mess your happiness up. What are you staying prepared for?" her grandfather asked.

"The hurt to come back so I can feel it, deal with it, and move on," she says as she lowers her head.

All eyes are on both Mo' and her grandfather.

"But why does it have to be that way. We know that you have been dealing with hurt, and you have been trying to hurt others in the process, but it's going to *stop* today. It's time to face the truth, stop with this disrespectful outburst, and move forward. Do you really like to hurt all the time?" He moves closer to her.

Mo' begins to cry. Through her tears, she says, "No, but that's all I know. You know how my mom was. We weren't ever happy… this feel's really strange," as she wipes her tears away.

"Let it feel strange until it becomes your norm," he assures Mo'. "Life will bring some hurt because that's life, but you have a choice whether you want to live out the hurt are grow from it as you move forward in happiness. You have us around you that are here to help, but we can't help you if you don't want to help yourself." He hugs her closer to him.

She looks up at all of us looking at her. In our own little way, we agree with what her grandfather has told her. She smiles back, and I do a sigh of relief as I blow my smores. I am hoping, wishing, and praying this is a start of happiness for her.

December—oh, how the months are moving so fast. This weekend Mo' has asked that we all come over for a sleepover. I don't have to work that Saturday, so that is cool. Má says she will let me drive with the girls. Yes, Má will be in the car. I'm so excited, more excited about the drive than anything else. Saturday comes. The gurls meet at my house, and we start to load the car.

"What are you doing?" Joz asks as she gets in the backseat.

"I'm driving to Mo's house," I say as I open the driver's side door.

"Hey na, gone head." Lee pushes me a bit as she gets in the backseat.

As we head to Mo's, the gurls are chatting it up and Má is texting. She looks over at me and says, "It's great over here in the passenger seat. I can get a lot done."

I give her that *Oh I know what you are thinking with what you just said quick* look.

We pull into Mo's driveway. She is standing on the porch waving, looking cold. We get our things. As we walk up to Mo', I wave bye to Má. She says as she waves out the window, "Tell Nathan and Racheal I said hello, and if they need anything, they know how to reach us."

I wave bye as I read between the lines, which means "Mo's grandparents betta not call!"

We go into the house, and Mo' has us place everything in the den, which is all set up. Their den has really pretty glass doors painted with what looks like roses, crosses, and sunflowers. Kind of kool. We place our stuff down.

Mo' says, "My house isn't as nice as Carmella's, but its mine."

"Gurl, bye!" I look over at her and wave my hand to dismiss the nonsense she just said.

We follow her into the kitchen where Mrs. Racheal is making snacks. Mr. Nathan hasn't made it home from work, I'm assuming. "You gurls can grab as you go. Dinner will be ready shortly. We are having nachos. Then I will be out your hair."

We all thank her in unison. I'm thinking to myself, *those nachos going to be so good?*

We head out the backyard to chill a bit, but wait…

"Gurl, you have a tether ball! Oh, come get your biscuits whooped!" I scream as I'm running to it. I grab the ball and hit Lee up first. I get her out in three hits.

Joz comes up, looks at Lee, and says, "Let me show you how it's done!" with a hip sway.

Lee walks off to stand over by Mo'. Mind you, yes, its cold outside, but who cares? I'm about to give them a whoopin' they have never felt. Joz is a little competition, but I get her out in five hits. LOL. Over comes Mo' as she says, "Take it easy on me. I never played this."

"Um, nope not going to happen," I say as I'm jumping up and down with excitement, also teasing Mo', putting the ball in her face all at the same time. "If I take it easy, you want ever learn," I say with determination in my eyes and voice. I hit the ball so hard it goes really fast Mo' didn't even try to hit it.

She said, "Man," as she watches the ball go around. "Too cold, inside we go."

We all laugh and make our way into the den, which has a fireplace. I didn't notice that before. Mo' gives us the rundown of how tonight will go. We will play games, gurl talk, and chill mostly. With Mo', you have to stay ready 'cause you never really know with her. She always has something up her sleeve. I have learned that about her.

We eat dinner. Ms. Racheal kept enough snacks out. We are right by the kitchen, so she let us know that we are free to have at it. As the night begins to wind down, we have pillow fights, play

Monopoly cards because Mo' wanted to kick Joz's biscuits, and Lee does everyone's nails and toes, including her own. She took pic of it all, and you already know, Joz started posting. She told us that she had been posting since the drive to Mo' house. We all look at each other with that *We should have known* look. No matter where Joz is and what she is doing, she is going to post about it on her chat and 'gram.

Ms. Racheal and Mr. Nathan comes to tell us good night. We say in unison, "Night." They head upstairs. It had to be midnight by now, and Mo' comes out to say "Hey, want to play light as a feather, stiff as a board."

We all look at each other, and Lee asks, "How do you play that?"

Mo' is explaining the game. I get this real eerie feeling, but I don't let the gurls know because I don't want to be the slumber-party popper. I just hide my feeling. We all agree to play.

Joz lies down first. Why, I don't know. We need her to record. But little did we know—well, I will get to that later. Mo' is at her head, and I and Lee are on the sides. Mo' stated we needed someone down at her feet, but we didn't have anyone. Now we are only supposed to place our fingertips under her on each hand. Based on whatever story, Mo' says Joz is supposed to float in the air.

Mo' has her hands on Joz's temple and begins to tell the story. "Highschool gurl comes in from track practice. She goes into the shower. As the water is falling down on her head and she gets relaxed, she feels something."

I'm looking at Lee like *Hey, this sounds very familiar*. She gives me that look like *Yelp*. Mo' has pulled Joz head back somewhat is that some sort of and right as she is about to say what it is.

We must have not been paying attention because Joz begins to float, and the only reason we know that is because Ms. Racheal opens the door and says, "What in the world!" as Joz falls to the pillows on the floor. "Mo'Lynn, what is going on?" Ms. Racheal snaps as she is holding her cup of whatever.

"Nothing, nothing, we wasn't doing nothin'." Mo' tries to sound innocent, but it's not working. Ms. Racheal is not buying it.

"If it's nothing you was doing, you don't mind me leaving this door open, and I will be sleeping on the couch so I can keep a good eye on you."

Mo' gives Ms. Racheal a look as if she could kill her.

"Now time to go to sleep," Ms. Racheal says as we all see her go lie on the couch.

We get in our sleeping bags, and I look over at Lee and whisper, "Ms. Racheal already had the couch made up to sleep on. You think she knew that Mo' would try something, and does she know everything we talked about?"

Lee responds with, "I don't know, but we betta go to sleep before she comes back in here."

We all go to sleep, as we thought, but leave it up to Joz saying she was going to get Mo' back, and that's what she meant. Mo' got up at about 3:00 a.m. to go into her room to do who knows what. Joz has one of those cameras that you can see if you slide it under the door. She recorded Mo' looking in the mirror, chanting with a book in front of her, with something in her hand that she keeps hitting really quick and with some fluid coming out. As Mo' was done, Joz snuck back down, got in her sleeping bag, and acted like she was asleep.

Later that morning, we woke up to a good-smelling breakfast with orange juice on the side. I look over at Joz, asking, "Did you get any sleep last night 'cause, honey, you got bags under your eyes for days?" She laughs a little bit.

After breakfast, we all get ready, and Má picks us up. As we go to the car, Mo' waves bye from the porch. She looks as if she really didn't want us to go. Ms. Racheal didn't come out to say anything to Má, so I guess what happens at the slumber party stays at the slumber party?

"So, gurls, how did it go?" Má ask us all.

"It went really good, Mrs. Carmel, really good." Joz gives this smile like *Yelp, so good I got her now.*

"That's nice." Má didn't look up from her phone.

I drop the gurls off one by one, then as we make it home and pull into the driveway, I place the car in park, Má asks, "How did it really go?"

I think to myself, *Don't you say nothing.* "It went good." I shrug 'cause I'm unsure of what to say.

"Nothing happened?" Má puts her phone down and gives me the look like *I already know, I just want to hear you say it.*

"Happened like what?" I try to look like *I don't know what she is talking about even though I do.*

"I'm asking you that, Carmella." Má's still giving me that look.

"Nope," I say as I pop the truck to get my stuff out.

Má is looking at me through the rearview mirror. I put the trunk down as she shuts the passenger-side door. She is still giving me that look as she touches my shoulder and we go in the house. As I'm walking behind her, my phone buzzes. I don't look at it right away 'cause I'm so nervous. I tell myself to check it when I get to my room.

# CHAPTER 15

I GO DROP ALL my laundry in the washroom to begin to wash it all. I head upstairs to take a shower and get ready to just chill out 'cause something very strange is going on. We didn't even go to youth group this morning. We all had thought we were going to go from Mo's grandparents' house and then leave with our parents.

After I get into my comfy clothes, I finally check my phone. It's a text from Lee. OUR MOTHERS KNOW WHAT HAPPEN LAST NIGHT AT MO'LYNN. JUST WANTED TO GIVE YOU A HEADS UP.

I say to myself, *Dang, should have checked my phone!* Now I'm going to be in trouble for not just going on ahead and telling Má. Dang! As soon as I drop my phone and head to my door to go tell on myself, there is a knock, and Má comes right on in. I'm thinking I betta gone head and tell her what happen since she already knows.

Before she could say anything, I went ahead and spilled it all. I explained how I didn't want to because I didn't want to be the snitch 'cause they do get stitches and what we did at Mo' house should stay at Mo's house. Ms. Racheal had already gotten on us about it. Má said that she understood, but what happened was very serious— more serious than we know—that was in the natural as well as in the spiritual realm, and it could affect us in ways we don't really under- stand right now. We prayed for everyone. Má got on me about lying to her, and I betta not ever do it again.

Má hugs me. I pat her back, but I am still in a world spin in my head. As Má gets up to leave, I get another text but from Joz. She had sent a group text with everything that she recorded last night.

GURL, YOU ARE SOMETHING ELSE, I text.

She replies, I TOLD YOU I WAS GOING TO GET HER. THERE IS PROOF ON THERE ABOUT HER PUTTING THAT FROG IN MY HEAD IN THE LOCKER ROOM.

Lee texted, NOPE. IT DOESN'T SAY WHAT WAS IN YOUR HEAD, AND EVERYONE KNEW ABOUT IT ONCE YOU MISSED SCHOOL, SO SHE COULD HAVE JUST BEEN REPEATING WHAT SHE HEARD.

ALL MAN. I DIDN'T THINK OF IT LIKE THAT. DANG! THAT'S OK THOUGH. CHECK OUT THE OTHER VIDEOS.

WHAT DO YOU PLAN ON DOING WITH THESE?" Lee texted back.

I'M GOING TO SHOW MY PARENTS, Joz texted back.

WAIT, I began to text. I THOUGHT THIS WAS GOING TO STAY BETWEEN US AND WE DEAL WITH IT.

HUH? WELL OUR PARENTS ALREADY KNOW FROM WHAT HAPPENED YESTERDAY. THEY ARE ALREADY IN THE LOOP. SO YES, I'M SHOWING MY PARENTS.

I think, *Did Joz rat us out or did Ms. Racheal tell on us or did both them tell?* Mannnn! I'm not going to ask Joz because I don't feel like dealing with her on that right now. The truth is coming out, so hey.

Lee chimes in. AND WHAT DO YOU THINK THEY ARE GOING TO DO?

I DON'T KNOW, Joz replied. BUT MO'LYNN HAS TO BE STOPPED BEFORE SHE GETS US ALL SERIOUSLY HURT.

NOW YOU ARE RIGHT ABOUT THAT. I HOPE SHE GETS THE HELP SHE NEEDS. I REALLY DO, Lee texted with concern. I text TTYL because this is too much for me and I need a break from it all.

I send a text to Ty to see if he can come over and chill and to let me know what happened in youth group. I really don't like missing it. As I wait for his reply, I go ask Má if it's kool for Ty to come over to chill a bit. She said it was okay. I know I did it backward. I was supposed to ask Má first, but hey, Ty hasn't even replied back yet. I do backward stuff most times, and besides, it gets done.

Ty replies back, MOST DEF. I send back, SEE YOU THEN.

I chill out on the porch because I'm still heated from everything that's going on until Ty comes over. He always brightens me up. Nope, I'm not going to tell him what happened, either. I'm still keeping it between the gurls. Just like they have a guy code, we have a gurls' code.

Ty gets dropped off. I tell him we will chill in the living room, too cold outside. He says okay and follows me into the house. I offer him some soda water and snacks. He is just sitting on the couch, staring at me. I look back and say, "Well?"

He throws some popcorn into his mouth. "Well what?"

"Don't play. Fill me in," I say as I rub my hands together with intensity.

"The message from youth group was, 'Do you know who you are?'"

"Wow, that's a good question, and it changes as we grow, right?"

"True." Ty nods as he sips his soda. "But your foundation, your core, should stay the same no matter what 'cause that's what you are created on. That's what you continue to build on."

"You know what? You are very smart dude." I took a bite from my sandwich.

"That's what you tell me." He pops his collar and winks at me.

"I know you get told that a lot." I playfully push him.

"It means more coming from you." Ty flirts a little. I know that he means every word, though.

After soda water and snacks, we played some cards, watched some TV, then dinner time came, and Ty had to go home. Dad asked if Ty needed him to drop him off. Ty said, "No, thanks. I like the walk. It's not that far." It really was just right up the hill, maybe ten to fifteen houses. It's cold out there, so Má sent him with some hot chocolate with a bunch of marshmallows. She texted Mrs. Claretha to let her know that Ty was walking home.

Monday, Monday, you came way too early. The weekend mood is still upon me. It totally feels like I'm dragging, and before I know it, I'm at the bus stop. Ty is standing there, listening to his music, and he knows when I'm about to come walk up 'cause he takes one out of his ear and says, "Good morning, gorgeous." I look at him very dazed with a half-smile. We get on the bus, take our seats, stop at Lee's stop, and on to school we go.

We enter homeroom, and Joz is just staring at Mo'. It is so funny 'cause you can see the seriousness or determination to get back, or is that what pre-revenge looks like? But Mo' pays her no attention at all. After homeroom comes lunch. I'm always starving around lunch time, or am I being dramatic? I am very hungry, though. We are all at the booth but Mo'. She doesn't even come sit with us, to which, at this point, I really don't even care. Let her keep them foolish vibes over there with her.

Joz shot us a text because she don't want the fellas to know what we are talking about. She let us know that her parents are meeting with Mo'Lynn's grandparents and she might just get kicked out of school. Lee texted back, HOLD UP. WHY?

—WHAT SHE DID HAPPEN ON SCHOOL GROUNDS.

—YOU NEED TO PROVIDE PROOF OF WHAT HAPPENED HERE IN ORDER FOR HER TO GET IN TROUBLE FOR WHAT SHE DID HERE, JOZ.

—WHY DOES IT FEEL LIKE YOU ARE TAKING HER SIDE? You can tell that Joz is feeling some type of way.

—MAN, LOOK GET OUT YOUR FEELINGS. YOU KNOW THAT I'M RIGHT. GET TO THE FACTS, REPORTER, Lee texted back with attitude of *I'm right, so deal with it.* I'm giving them both QRZ looks. Lunch is over, two classes, then back to the big yellow bus. To my surprise, Má has showed up at school, so I drive Lee and Ty home. Then I drive to work. I'm loving it, feels so adultish.

Back at work, and guess who strolls in? Mo'. After all that she had pulled, she shouldn't be able to come back up in here. She has this demeanor about her that she does no wrong, that she can do what she wants she doesn't care who it affects. She is going to do what she wants when she wants. I'm clearing off the tables, and she walks right past me like she doesn't see me. I keep wiping the tables then I sit at a booth to clean the trays off. She sits at the booth right in front of me so that I can see her. At this point, it's just a stare-off. She is eating her burger with an attitude. Why, I don't know. She is snatching her fries out to her mouth and drinking her soda water. I'm giving her the look of *Whatever you got, bring it on, sista,* as I continue to wipe the trays.

She finishes her food, walk past me just enough to bump my foot with hers, then throws her scraps in the trash, including the tray. Now I'm about to say something. "Um, did you forget something?"

She looks at me with her hand on the door as she pushes it to go out. "Um, nope."

That heffa really gets on my nerves, I tell ya. My manager comes by and hands me the tray and says, "I suggest you stay away from her." Then she heads over to speak to a customer. I think to myself as I'm putting the trays up, *How am I supposed to do that when we are pretty much always around each other somehow?*

The end of my shift has come, and yelp, time for this chickadee to drive our biscuits home. I get in the driver's seat. Má is on her cell phone texting. I look over at her as I buckle my seatbelt and say, "Aren't you a little too old to be texting?" as I laugh.

"So you want to go there, huh?" She tips her head toward me but doesn't look up from her phone. "So how was work?"

"Mo' came in and didn't say a word. We did the staring thang. We both knew what was going on, and then her rude biscuits threw the tray in the trash and bumped my foot. My manager got it out and told me to stay clear of Mo'."

"Wait a minute. Isn't your manager one of the youth advisors at the church?" Má asks, putting her phone on her lap. She doesn't give me time to answer back. "Oh no, she should have told you why she thinks you should stay away for your clarity. Carmella, some people need us more than they know. Now, we don't let them keep doing us wrong. We do stand in the gap for them and pray for them. Just be there for Mo'Lynn if she ever needs is all. She really needs someone. She just really don't know and keeps fighting those that try to help."

"Yes, ma'am," I say, 'cause to be honest I don't even understand what my Má is talking about, but she is already fired up, and I really don't feel like getting to even know what she means.

We get home, and I really don't have nothing to do, but I tell ya what, I don't want to think no more on this day or Mo'—that gurl is so draining. I finished my homework on my lunch break. I don't want to hit the gurls up with what happened 'cause then Joz will get all fired up. I will journal about it just to get it off my mind.

We are already in the third week of December by this time. This month is going by quick. I don't have work, so I go to ask Má when will be leaving to go to the cabin with Ty and his family. As I sit on the bar stool, Má is once again cooking up something that just takes you from this country to another one. Má lets me know that we are waiting on Dad to know how long we will be there. I look down to straighten the mat. I move a bit and say, "I'm really looking forward to going. It's something new, and we haven't done any of those things that Ty say we will be doing."

"I know, baby. It's a family affair," Má assures me.

I head back up to my room to finish journaling and chill out, wishing from my window.

# CHAPTER 16

CHRISTMAS IS THIS WEEK, and yes, we are headed down to the cabin to be there for about two weeks. This is going to be so much fun. Since we drove up a little later than Ty and his parents, I had the whole backseat all to myself. If we had gone with everyone else, Ty would have wanted to ride with us, but sometimes, I still just like it when it's just me.

We get to the cabin, and it's gorgeous. To my surprise, Joz and her parents are here, and so is Teli and his dad. I thought it was just going to be Ty's family and mine, but hey, I should have thought betta. All the parents have their own rooms, Joz and I are in one room, and Teli and Ty in another. It all worked out. Lee and her family are in beautiful Hawaii for the holidays. I love the log cabin and the smell of it all. From the outside, you see that it's a log mansion, but once you walk in, it's like you are in a luxury home. We even have a chef. Why, I don't know 'cause Má always almost does all the cooking. Well, this can give her a break. There are plenty of activities to do, from skiing to tubing, to sliding and more. I watch the snow fall, setting on the window sill—it's so relaxing.

TY walks up and whispers in my ear, "I told ya."

I look back at him. He is smiling from ear to ear with his hot chocolate with tons of marshmallows in one hand and the other hand on my shoulder. He goes to say, "We have a lot planned for these cabin weeks. New Year's is the best, though." You can see the excitement in his eyes.

"I do love the lights. Don't know why, but I do," I say as I sip my hot chocolate with no marshmallows, thank you. "What are the plans?" I ask Ty, who by this time has had a seat right next to me.

"Nope, nope, nope! You will see when you see." Ty nods like he just said something worthy.

"Let's go find the rest of the crew," I suggest.

As we are walking down the hall, we come into this room with recliner seats and a projector screen.

"'Bout time you show up, we been waiting." Joz looks over the side of the recliner with her hand and mouth full of popcorn.

Teli chimes in with "Not really" as nonchalant as he can.

"What movie we going to watch?" I sat in the recliner next to Joz. She shrugs, still smacking.

"An action movie!" Teli says. "I picked it out myself." Mind you, he is a big comic fan, so no telling what he has picked to watch. So is most of the men and the youngsters on this vacay.

Right as the movie was about to start, the parents joined us. It is so nice to spend quality time like this. I look over and see Mr. John, who is all by himself. He seems unbothered by it.

As the movie came to end, everyone headed to their rooms. We are not even in our bunk when Joz looks down and say, "Hey, C, you sleep?"

"Trying to go. Why." I fluff my pillow.

"I've been thinking a lot about the Mo'Lynn stuff, and I think it might be time that I just go confront her and let her know what I have on her."

"And do you think that is a good idea?" I lie with my eyes closed, hoping she gets the hint. "What would you do if she came to confront you if the places were switched?"

"You right, you right. I will think more on what's best of thangs to do."

Before I knew it, what I was thinking came out my mouth. "Please hear me good. I don't want to be talking about Mo' on this trip at all. To be honest, I don't even want to have to think about her when she is mentioned." Don't even know if I heard what Joz had said as I was talking.

"I hear ya. Good nite." In no time she was out with a soft snore.

The next morning, we all head downstairs for breakfast. The men are cooking breakfast this morning. I'm like, yes, it's great to see my dad in the kitchen. There is a nice spread laid out on the table. We all sit and say grace, then we began to chow down. I get this feeling of just warmth and love.

After breakfast, we are off to do some snow-tubing. It's so cold out here good thang I brought me some gloves as I was about to leave. We all have our tubs, and we go up this conveyor belt, and then down we go. Don't know how many times we done it, but each time was more exhilarating than the last.

We can even hear our parents screaming and enjoying themselves. There is a place for "all things hot," it was called. As I began to walk over to get me a hot cocoa, I hear a voice.

"Hold up. Don't leave me. I'm coming with you." Joz is shouting and running to catch up to me.

I laugh and say to her, "You almost fell on your biscuits."

She laughs back. "Yeah, I did."

We get our hot cocoa, and they taste so good. Joz tries the peppermint and cherry marshmallows in hers. The young girl asks me if I wanted any. I told her, "I don't eat marshmallows, but thank you." Once we finish, we both look at each other, knowing what we are saying without using words. We trash our cups and head right on back to the snow-tubing. We tubed so long that we forgot about lunch. By the time we made it back to the cabin, we were so hungry everyone's bellies had started rumbling. Good thang Má is always prepared. She had some sausage, meat, and veggies stewing in the Crock-Pot and rice in the rice cooker. No one even got out their clothes—we all ran straight to the kitchen to get some of the good grub that we could taste just from the smell.

After pretty much dinner, we all have freshened up, so we start to play cards. Our parents are playing spades, and oh yes, it's gets heated. We crack up, laughing at them because it's all just a card game, but not with the parents—they go all in. My parents and Ty parents are playing spades, and Joz parents and Teli's dad are playing dominos. Both tables are heated. They are so into it we have stopped our game to go see what's all the fuss about. We all keep going from table to table. The boz, of course, got snacks in their hand as they go back and forth. Just don't see how they can eat so much, especially Teli—he is always eating.

As Joz and I sit on the back of the couch, the parents are still at it. "Okay"—I look over at Joz—"I'm going to watch a little TV." I slide down the front of the couch and grab the remote off the table.

She turns, looks at me with her arms folded on the back of the couch, and says, "How with all this noise?"

"I will read the captions." I smile.

She turns back over, props herself to her comfort, as she enjoys watching the parents in their game. I find me a reality TV show to watch. To be honest, I'm excited the parents, especially Má, are into their game 'cause my parents don't like me watching TV. I don't understand why; it's just entertainment.

My show comes to an end, so I turn the TV off. The parents are still at it. I turn around with my knees on the couch and keep watching them laughing, arguing in a good way, and going at it like they are kids. Really kool to watch the parents have a great time as they just let it all hang out. They are having so much fun makes you want to join right on in. They must have played way into the night, and I must have fallen asleep on the couch. I get up briefly and see Joz on the couch with me, Teli on the couch to the left, and Ty on the couch to the right. The parents must have really been in a good mood because they let us be down here sleeping together. I just lie back on down and go back to sleep.

We wake up to the warm smell of fresh fruits, pancakes, waffles, eggs, bacon, and sausage. There are freshly squeezed orange juice, apple juice, and water. Our mothers, as they are cooking, they are having their mimosa. LOL. I get up off the couch with a huge yawn.

"You look ok when you first get up." I look over to my right, and Ty is chillin' but looking right at me.

"Really," I say. I don't feel embarrassed or nothing that he has seen me before I brushed my face and washed my teeth. Hahaha, I did the backward thang again. After breakfast and cleanup, I say,

"What happen to the chef?" No one says anything, and we are out the door to another adventure.

It's ski day. I don't know how to ski, but I'm going to try. They have ski lessons and a section just for beginners. Our parents are long gone. Didn't even know my parents knew how to ski. Teli and Ty drop Joz and I off to the beginner's area, and they go off to ski with the parents.

"Joz, we are the only two that don't know how to ski, man." I'm trying to hold on to her, so I don't fall over.

"I guess so." She looks at me as she is adjusting her boots.

"If we learn really fast, then we can be out there with everyone else." I get my sticks and try to balance.

"Nope, you can. I'm going to stay right here."

Even though I don't want to, I agree with her. There is no way we can learn that fast, anyway. I can't focus on the lesson because I'm too busy watching everyone else doing their thang. The boz has went by us, I can't even count the number of times. Every time they zoom by, they throw up a hand. I'm like *Really* for real. Then I look over at Joz, and she is having the time of her life without a care in the world. In my frustration, I'm trying to have a good time, but I'm not because I want to be out there going all fast with everyone else. After I make peace with myself, I began to have fun, but then it's about time to go. Time always flies when you are having fun, which I didn't get to have enough of. I wasted time, but it's all good 'cause we will come back, then I'm really going to enjoy myself.

After the skiing is over, we head to the ski lift to do our own tour. As you know, Joz is taking pic and writing down something every chance she gets, then she posts. I like to take it all in then go write about it because I don't want to miss nothing. That's why I like Joz because we are different but have some similarities. Besides, with all her photo taking, I can look at the pics just in case I forget something. We get off our tour, and it looks like we wasn't paying attention because it has landed us where all the advanced skiers are. We both look at each other, and I grab her shoulders and say, "We can do one are two thangs. We can just go down like we are pros, are we can wait for another lifter to come to take us down."

"We can just sit here and watch all the skiers and boarders," Joz says as she is taking pic.

We sat down to watch. No sooner than yelp, the boz come up and ask us what we are doing. I don't even look their way. Joz replies, "We are chillin', just watching everyone."

"It would be cooler if you join." Teli winks at her.

"We can't ski like that. We not ready." She is still taking pic.

"Maybe you will be before we leave." Teli begins to board down.

"Really." Joz doesn't take her eye from the lens.

As the boz head down, I'm thinking to myself, *I so want to get there. It's sure do look like so much fun.* Whenever we come back, I will let the instructor know that I'm no longer a beginner. I want to go to the moderate section.

Joz looks over to me and asks, "You ready to go? I have gotten a lot of pics, and its getting really cold."

Just as I'm about to say "Sure," a lifter comes, and Joz hops on. I'm right next to her. I look at her and ask, "Oh you was just going to leave a sista, huh?"

She laughs. "Naw, nothing like that, but I didn't want to wait on another one. It's cold, man."

We both laugh so hard. Before we knew it, we are back at the beginner's area. We walk over to get hot cocoa inside the lodge as we find a window to continue to watch everyone. As QRZ as it is, we can see everyone from the window.

I say, "Man, we should have just come in here to look."

"Maybe, but I wouldn't have been able to get these good pics that I took up top," Joz says as she is looking through the pics she just took.

"I guess," I mope a little.

We continue to people-watch until everyone is ready to go home.

Once we get back to the cabin, everyone is pretty much beat. We eat the delicious three-meats-and-veggie stew Má had brewing all day and everyone hit the sack, even Joz, and I'm thinking to myself, *We didn't do that much. Why is she so sleepy?*

Since I can't sleep, I go downstairs, make me some hot chocolate, and sit in the circle frame window. I just look out at the stars as the snow falls, and I can see the moon, thinking of everything and nothing in between taking sips of the hot chocolate. Next thing I know, its morning. I have a blanket spread over me, but I'm still in the same spot I was in last night when I couldn't sleep. I smell freshly baked muffin, eggs, turkey bacon, sausage, biscuits, and freshly squeezed orange juice. There is apple juice and water laid out. I sit straight up just to take the smell in.

Mrs. Fisher walks by with coffee in her hand. "Good morning! Did Joz keep you up with her snoring."

"Oh no, ma'am. I couldn't sleep, so I came down, made me some hot chocolate, and then now I'm talking to you."

She laughs, and I hear Má and Ms. Claretha laughing as they are setting the table.

"I guess you betta go and get yourself together before you know who comes down." They all look at me.

"Má, really?" I say with a little embarrassment in my voice.

I head upstairs to get myself together. As I'm making my way upstairs, I can hear everyone trying to decide what we will do today.

I say, "I thought we are supposed to go on a tour."

"Who said anything about a tour." Dad looks over the top of his glasses.

"I do remember someone saying something like that," Ms. Claretha says.

"What kind of tour you ladies thinking?" Sr. questioned.

"Why it has to be us ladies?" Mrs. Fisher lifts one eyebrow.

Mr. John just laughs, then he says, "there are some really good touring sites. Since its cold, we can try to find one indoors."

"The only indoor tours they have is the winery, and Carmella's not going to nothing like that." Má let everybody know.

"You got a point there," Mr. Fisher agrees.

"We have to find something to do. I don't want to be sitting up in here with these oldies all day," Joz chimes in like she has an idea but don't even say nothing. I laugh and look at Ty, whom we can always count on to find something to do.

"There is a game room and a movie theater that we all can go to while you all are at the winery." Sr. gives Ty some dab. His mom shakes her head.

"Wait, wait, wait," Dad says, "who say we men want to go to a winery?"

"Chill, dude." Mr. John hits Dad on the shoulder. "At the winery, while he is reading from his phone, there is a cigar joint we can chill out at."

"Now you are talking," Dad agrees.

We all pile up in two different SUVs. Now if I have had my license, it could have been all of us teens in one and the parents in another. Since I just have a permit, Sr. drives us and drops us off, then the parents head off to the winery and cigar joint.

The boz are in hog heaven. I'm not the gamer type, but I betta start quick because everyone is having a great time and I'm standing here like a fish out of water.

Ty comes over and grabs my hand. "Come on, we will start at the b-ball game, then we will go to all the other stuff."

As we get to the game, Joz and Teli were there waiting. It's a row of b-ball machines. We are all against each other. You think you already know who will win 'cause they both play ball, but they don't—Joz wins. Yes, we were all surprised.

Teli looks at Joz as he leans up against the game. "You know we let you win, right?"

"Don't even give me that." She snaps her fingers and sway her body to bump Teli.

"Okay, let's go again. This time by fifteen points."

Ty says, "Dude, you was so busy looking over at Joz, that's why you lost."

"Whatever, man." Teli gets the ball in his hand.

After that b-ball game, they go over to play Pac-man. As they walk off, Ty tells Teli, "Don't be upset," still laughing harder this time at him. We must have played every game in the place together and separately. Before we knewit, it was time for the movie.

We grab our snacks as we take our seats to watch some animated comic, which is okay with me. It was about a kid, then there was fighting to save the day. Blah, blah, blah. Once the movie is over, I check my phone. There is a text from Má that says they will be here shortly to pick us up. There was another text from Mo', which was a surprise. I didn't even check it, said to myself, I don't have time for her shenanigans."

"Whose shenanigans?" Joz asked.

"I thought I said that in my head."

"Nope, it came right on out your mouth." Joz is looking at me, waiting to get her answer to her question.

"Má says they are on their way to pick us up."

"Don't try to change the subject." Joz looks at me out of the corner of her eye this time.

We make our way to a booth where we can see the parents once they pull up. I show Joz the text on my phone from Mo'. The boz are smacking on something and playing thumb wars. I'm like, *Really, that is a second grader game.* Boz will be boz.

"Are you going to read it?" Joz taps my phone to try and read what it says.

I jack my phone and say, "*No.*"

"K." Joz give me that look like *You betta 'cause you know she is always up to something.*

We see the parents pull up, and we head to the SUVs. Sr. ask us how things went once he drives off to head back to the cabin. We all started talking at once, interrupting each other, talking over each other, laughing, and thangs. Sr. says, "That well, huh?" We are still going on and on.

As we make it back to the cabin, Joz is watching me with that weird look. I give her a *Leave me alone* stare, and she stares back *Nope*.

# CHAPTER 17

Two DAYS HAVE WENT by, and nope, I still haven't checked the text, mainly because I don't want to be bothered. Everyone decides just to chill and do whatever around the cabin. We started our snowman contest, and right as we get into the middle of building, who pulls up? Yelp, you guessed right—it's Mo'. Once I seen her grandparents' car pull up, I was in utter shock, so shocked that I could see Joz's lips moving but couldn't hear nothing she was saying. When I finally came to, the parents were already greeting them and welcoming them into the cabin. Once the cabin's front door was shut, I reached into my pocket to see the text. As I began to read to myself, Joz is reading it out loud.

GAME ON HEFFAS, Mo' had sent.

"Why would she send that, and what do she mean?" Joz asked sternly.

"What is she doing here and who invited them?" I look Joz straight in the eyes. As I was saying that to her, I was thinking, *I hope Má didn't.*

We walk in the house together, and as I close the door, I hear Má say, "I hope you don't mind. I invited them over just for the weekend."

Everyone looked in agreement. I think to myself, *That's three whole days.* This chick is always up to something. I hope she doesn't think she is sleeping in the room with Joz and me. I must have had a strange look on my face because I feel a hand placed on my shoulder. I look up, and it's dad. He looks at me and say, "You know how your mother is. They had nowhere to go. Remember it's only for the weekend."

I whisper to him, "But, Dad, that's three whole dazes and you—"

Before I could finish, he just says, "Be nice."

They settle in, and of course, Má has set up Mo' a bed in our room. I love Má and all, but goodness, man, it was so much fun till Mo' got here. She is always doing something she has no buziness with. As I go into a rant in my mind, Joz comes and sits on the bottom bunk and places her arm around my shoulder. "Hey, chill out. You have to learn to have a poker face. She can see you sweating," she says as she wipes the sweat off my forehead.

"Shud we all can."

We both laugh. "It's not funny," I say, aggravated.

"It is because you are trippin'." Joz chuckled.

"You haven't seen me fall nowhere." I roll my eyes.

"Uh-huh," Joz responded with one eyebrow up. "Like I told you, we going to get her back. She is here for three days, so let's make the best of it. Just follow my lead." She stands up. I just look at her.

Then Mo' walks in, and she begins to put her things away. As she is doing that, she is talking to us like we are friends. Joz is engaging her. I'm just watching.

"We are going to have a great time this weekend. What's the plans?" Mo' keeps putting her stuff away.

"We are having a snowman competition, which we need to get back to." Joz hits me on my knee.

"Kool. Who's team am I on?" Mo' asked.

"The teams were divided evenly until the fifth wheel showed up. So now we just have to see." I flared my nose.

"It's like that?" Mo' stood there with both her hands upward and her shoulders lifted some.

I walked right past her, slapping one of her hands, and headed down the stairs.

The boz and the parents are in the living room.

"Are we going to get back to the competition are what?" Teli says.

"How are we going to do that with the fith wheel? I mean a fifth person?" I ask. I don't look Má's way, but I can feel her staring, burning a hole in the side of my head.

"I must've been the seventh wheel until they came," Mr. John says as he laughs.

Sr. touches Mr. John on the shoulder and laugh as he says, "I will get on the boz team, then it will be even. I want do much of the physical work, but I can delegate."

We all agree and head back outside to the front. As I'm heading out the door, Má grabs my arm and talks through her teeth, "Be nice." I look and then head out the door.

"Since I'm coming into what was already being done, I will just follow your lead." Mo' looks at me like *Don't try nothing 'cause I'm ready for ya.*

"That would be best." I give her the look *Now come on with it.*

Joz and I are placing the head on top of the body. "Do you have any suggestions?" Joz asked as she shoulder-bumped me.

"Naw, I have never done this before." Mo' tries to give a sad look.

"Mo'Lynn, really, everyone has been around snow," Joz counters.

"I didn't say I wasn't around snow. I just never built a snow-man," Mo' replies.

"Oh well, first time for every thang, huh. Even though you haven't done it, by seeing what you see now, you might have some suggestions." Joz sounds really friendly.

Mo' just shrugs her shoulder. I think to myself, *So why you wanted to even get on the team if you weren't going to do nothing?*

We began to put the buttons. Now we put big, huge rhine-stones for the eyes. The nose was a rose-gold buckle. She had an afro with a scarf that could blow in the wind. Don't forget her bling-bling shades that are hooked tightly to the scarf.

"You gurls not playing, huh?" I hear Dad say.

"She gets that side from me." Má has to let everyone know how proud she is. "Who would have ever imagined it?"

Mrs. Fisher gives that look like *Yeah, we know*, as she laughs. Mr. Fisher and Dad look at each other and say, "Joz and Carmella!" as they laugh.

The boz has a regular snowman. Theirs was a boy, of course, and he has on an ugly sweater, button eyes, and a carrot for a nose, with a baseball cap on.

"A rabbit is going to come and eat that nose right off." Joz points out, laughing.

"No, it is not." Teli turns. Seems it looks to be, he is a little upset.

Ty place his hand on Teli's shoulder. "Don't let her get to ya man." You can see Teli's chest puff up. LOL.

As we make our way back into the house to get warmed up, Mr. John tells us who won, which we already know.

"Gurls rule, like seriously?" Mo' shouts and dances around. "What is the prize?"

I think to myself, *Here she goes.* Mr. John says, "No physical prize. The prize is the fact that you won."

"That's stupid!" Mo' snaps.

Before I knew it, my rant came out my head straight through my mouth. "Okay, heffa, I been tired of you. You not going to mess this up," I shout as I poke on her head of puffy hair.

We began to tussle and wrestle around for a bit. The boz try to break us up, but they are not strong enough and get caught up with us. I hear in the midst of the chaos, "Let them get it out. It's been a long time coming." It was Mo' grandfather. By this time, I'm slinging her all around by her hair, shirt, and anything else I can sling her by. She has gotten me 38 degrees hot.

Once the dads break us up, the boz are laughing 'cause the two of us look a hot mess. Hair is all QRZ looking. Mo' shirt is torn. Both our noses are bleeding.

Má comes over and say, "I hope you both got it all out!" as she hands us a towel. "You two going to clean this mess yawl made too."

Ms. Claretha says, "I got it. They have done enough." She raises her cup as a toast and gives a wink.

"Gone upstairs and get cleaned up, babes," Mo' grandmother says to us.

"I will help and ref if they start up again." Joz walks behind us, but you can hear her laugh.

"They betta not 'cause next time, oh you know what's coming!" Má is not having it.

I go in one bathroom and Mo' goes into the other to get cleaned up. Joz stands out in the hall to watch out. As we get done, we head back downstairs for lunch, then in the SUVs to go look at the ice-sculpting competition, which none of us have been to but Ty and his fam. Ty says we are all going to love it.

As we get there, it's not just a competition—it's a winter carnival. Really kool from what I can see as we park. We get to the competition, and I'm in awe. The sculptors that these people are doing are mind-blowing. Ty leans over and says to me, "This competition takes like up to four days. They have their partners, and they go at it. Some people watch all these days, some come in and out."

"You telling me people sit here for four days?" I'm just amazed.

"Yelp." Ty folds his arms.

"I want to watch."

We find a seat and begin to watch. The competitors have saws, chisels, and they even have tools I didn't know the name of or even knew existed for that matter. They were moving as if they were dancing to a song that they were the only ones attuned too. As I watched, I found myself wanting to dance with them. I was full of excitement and anticipation of what the outcome would be. I was trying to figure it out before seeing the end project, which was days away.

I could see one group was building the Eiffel Tower. It had beautiful lights going in and out, but if you look closer right there in the middle, they had built a platform, and you see just three people that looked like a couple getting married. Then another group built what looked like a mansion, and each room that it displayed had something very unique and very eye-catching. The way they opened the sculpture so that you could see everything was amazing. Another group built this garden-type thing, if I'm looking correctly, but maybe not. It was a blooming huge rose with beautiful colors, but it had little people, I think, doing different things on the petals. Now I see why it takes days because everything is so very particular and precise.

I must have been engrossed with watching them when I hear Ty ask me if I like to go around and see what else they have at the carnival. I look over to him and ask, "How long we been here?"

"You have been here about two hours. I left to meet up with everyone else and tell them where we are."

I get up but keep thinking I don't want to leave 'cause then I'm going to miss out on something. But I follow Ty as he leads the way. I touch him and say, "We must stop back by here before we leave." He says okay.

By this time, we meet up with everyone, and they are at another competition, one that I really don't care for. It's a pie-eating contest, and I give everyone a QRZ look, but no one cares. *I could have stayed where I was*, I say to myself with my head down. Look, who is up there in the contest—it's Mo'. This just got interesting. Don't know if I want her to win or lose, but I'm going to watch to see which one it's going to be. That gurl sure can pack away some pie. She is on the fourth one, and these are regular-size pies. All the competitors got pie everywhere, all over their faces—because you can't use your hands, and pie scraps on the table.

Mo' placed third. That was kool to watch. She did really good. We all congratulate her, then we go on to playing games. It's that time to leave, and as we are walking, I shout, "Wait. I wanted to go back by the sculptor competition."

Má says, "We are coming back tomorrow. Everyone is pretty tired. It's time to go."

"Can I just stay?" I whine a bit.

"Don't be ridiculous." Má snaps.

Back to the cabin we go. I'm real mad now 'cause I wanted to go back and see what was happening. Ty must have seen my face 'cause as we get out the SUV, he tells me, "Tomorrow is the last day, so when we go back, I will sit with you the whole time so you can see who wins."

"Thank you. I'm not in to seeing who will win. I want to see the work they are doing."

We both walk in the cabin. We all have stew and just chill out in the warmth.

Má calls me up to their room. It must be something very important.

"You have fun today?" Dad asked.

"Yeah." I have a seat on the end of the bed.

Má gives me that look like *Just yeah?*

"Yes, sir," I said as I folded my hands.

"I have to leave out early in the morning for work, but I should be back before the trip is over." Dad tries to speak with assurance.

"I thought you took off so we could have a family vacay?" I look sad.

"I did, but something has come up, and I must go back in to handle it, then I will be back as soon as I'm done. No more being a champion boxer, either, young lady," Dad says with a laugh.

I look at him with the *Really* look. Má grabs both our hands, says a prayer for Dad to have safe travel and grace and all that good stuff, then we all say amen. Then I leave the room and shut the door.

That night was just a regular night. We had homemade popcorn, Icee, and snacks. We watch all different kinds of movies 'til everyone went to sleep. The next day, Dad leaves early that morning. He leaves with Mo' and her grandparents. They will take him by the house to get his gear, then he will go handle business.

Sunday came right on time. I was so happy to see Mo' leave. The bad thing is, they all were gone before I even woke up. Má lets me know what all happened and how things are going to go down from this point. As we chill on the couch, I ask, "So will we go see the end of the competition tonight at the carnival?"

"Yes, we are." Má pats my back. As she leaves, I see a sadness in her eyes. I know she didn't want Dad to leave. I didn't, either, but he has to work. We are both thankful, though, that he was able to come and spend the time that he did. He said that he would make it back, so it's all good.

As lunch came around, we all made sub sandwiches. There were all kinds of meats, cheeses, tomatoes, lettuce, peppers, unions, and breads, with different sauces and dressing to place on it. Oh, don't forget the pickles. After lunch, we pretty much just lounge around. I came back to the room, and Joz was seating in the top bunk reading something.

"Hey, chick, what you are reading?" As I touch her knee, she jumps a bit.

"Something your friend left on my pillow." Joz doesn't even look my way.

"What you mean?" I ask. She hands me the paper without even moving from her position.

As I began to read the letter, Mo' is at it again. This is what the letter said.

> I was the one who put the frog in your head in the locker room. I haven't liked you since I first laid eyes on you. Then when you got so QRZ over me throwing your phone in the fire, I really had it out for you. I had planned on doing way more to you, but since I'm leaving, and you want see me again, I decided that I would let you know because I know you can't do anything about it.—Mo'Lynn

I just looked up at Joz with my mouth wide open. She looked back at me and said, "I knew she did it, and now here is the proof." Joz points to the letter.

"Are you going to show these to your parents?" I try to hand her the paper, but she is on a rant.

"Then she is leaving. So you do all this to me, and then you think you are just going to leave?" Joz is angry as she jumps from the top bunk. She didn't even hear the question I asked her. She starts pacing back and forth, babbling and chasing ideas out of her head.

I just sit on the bottom bunk with the letter still in my hands, waiting for her to finish whatever it is until she figures it out. She betta cause tonight we are going to the competition, and I don't want to be dealing with this while I'm watching it. Leave this mess right here. She paces a few more minutes, then decides that right now she is not going to tell her parents because this might be another trick. Mo' might just have told her all this to see if she would tell. We are just going to wait until if and when she leaves. Má likes to throw parties, so we will wait and see if she talks about throwing a going-away for them.

# CHAPTER 18

THAT NIGHT, WE HEAD off to the competition, which is a great distraction for Joz because of the letter she got. We make it right on time. There is room for all of us to sit on the bench on the second row. The sculptures are amazing. The winning sculpture, which surprised us all, was this one I'm going to try to do justice as I describe it. In the middle, it had a heart with crystal-like style with different colors coming through by way of standing and/or positioning the sculpture. Then it had something like a road that went circling around with a few hills. It had people riding from tricycles to a motorcycle. Every time a hill came, the people would change. Then right after the last hill, it was a couple that went through the heart and came out sitting on a swing chair, holding hands and looking into each other's eyes.

As I kept looking, I figured it out that they grew from childhood love to the lasting love of sitting on the swing. That team took us through a short story using the ice sculpture. We are all still trying to figure out how they got the movement and how the couple goes up through the heart without any wheels or nothing. Leave it up to Ty.

"Now there has to be some kind of engineering that I haven't quite researched yet because that was amazing," Ty says inquisitively.

"Why don't you just go and ask the team that, then you will have your answer?" I said.

"Nope, not going to happen. I'm going to figure it out. Then maybe next year I will get in the competition," he replies with his thinking cap on.

"You know, Son"—Sr. touches Ty's shoulder—"you are going to have to practice all year for a competition like that."

"Right on, Dad, I'm up for the challenge." Ty gives Sr. some dab. "You know that means—"

Sr. didn't get to finish as Ty interrupted him. "Yelp already working on it."

We walk around the carnival some more. Ride the big, huge Ferris wheel. Go to the bomber cars. Even though its cold out here, it's not as bad as I thought because I'm bundled up pretty good. I have on heated pad, socks, long john, gloves, bubble coat, sweater underneath the coat, jeans, and earmuffs. Yeah, this chick gets cold, but I'm so warm now.

"I don't want this to even end," Ty says as he puts his arm around my shoulders, and before I could respond, Teli throws his arm off and says, "Stop with all that."

We all laugh. We head over to the house of mirrors on to the next ride. Joz and I don't get on, but as we wait for the boz to get off, I look over at her. "Hey chickadee, you have been super quiet. You not letting that letter get to you, are ya?" I bump her shoulder with my arm.

"To be honest, yeah, just a little bit," Joz says nervously.

I just look at her 'cause I'm thinking, *All this time you wanted your answer. You got it. Now you all quiet.* Well, I thought I was thinking it 'cause Joz responded with, "You right. I just didn't think it would come like this. She has to be up to something still, you know. You can't trust Mo'Lynn at all."

"What are you going to do about it?" I ask.

"Don't know, but something will come to me. I know it will."

As Joz finishes what she is saying, the boz come off the roller-coaster. We all get a text to meet the parents. We head to the SUVs, and before you know it, cabin, here we are. As we enter the cabin, Joz is still puzzled. We had been having so much fun with all the activities that we had totally forgotten about Christmas. It is only not even a couple of days away. Time flies when you are having fun.

I go around the cabin looking for Má. She is upstairs in her room, sitting on the bed, reading something. "Má,'" I call as I open the door to her room.

She looks up. "Yes, sweetness."

163

"What are we going to do about Christmas? It's only a couple days away," I asked as I sat down next to her on the bed.

"To be honest, I haven't even thought much about it. How about we get everyone together and see what we all come up with?"

"Great idea, Má," I say.

I get up to go round everyone together. I look back in concern as I close the door behind me. I go screaming through the house in every room. "Hey, come downstairs in the living area. I want to ask you all something."

Everyone makes their way into the living area. I'm standing as everyone is sitting, like I'm about to give an inaugural speech or something. A thought cloud forms in my head, you never know, and I smile to myself. Back to the thangs at hand. "Christmas is only a couple days away what would you guys like to do?"

Ty is the frist to say something, as is most of the time. "We don't do gifts, per se. We vacay with each other—that's a gift all in itself. We usually just chill out with each other, eat, and play games."

"That sounds kool to me," Teli says as he munches on his Chex Flex. Mr. John gives him a look.

"No gifts, huh?" Joz ask as she cocks her head to the side.

Mrs. Fisher says, "Here she goes" with a laugh. "This is your Christmas present—being here this time. We need to start some new traditions, anyway. We buy you stuff you don't fool with after a while. The only thing that you keep up with that we got you is that phone. Which by the way, you are on it just about 24/7. What else do you really want and are need?" Mrs. Fisher's eyes get a little big. It looks so funny. As we laugh, I'm thinking to myself, *Since we want be buying any presents then*—before I knew it, the words were coming out my mouth. "How about we make gifts for everyone this Christmas?"

"Make? Make like what?" Joz is still in her *I want gifts* mood with her *I don't know* motions going on.

I keep talking like I don't hear her. "Make something memorable. We have done so much on this trip so far. We have a couple of days—we can do this. This is my most favorite time of year."

Everyone starts to look at each other in agreement.

"To make it just a little bit more interesting, how about we make it into a competition." Teli placed the last handful of Chex Flex in his mouth.

"With gifts?" Joz has attitude. "How we going to do that?"

We all tell her she is too crunck, but we also don't pay her too much mind, either.

"How about we come up with a theme, and you have to make your gifts from that?" Má states.

"It will only be the kiddos's in this?" Ms. Claretha asked.

Sr. says, "Let's do ya one betta. We are going to split you guys up in two teams. Ty and Carmella and then Teli and Joz."

"We are going to kick your butt." Joz points at us. Now all of a sudden, she is interested.

I give her that look like *Are you more interested because it's a competition or because you get to be with Teli, your secret crush?* She looks back at me and nods with a smile to let me know she knows and that's her answer.

"We don't have time to waste," I say as I grab Ty's hand.

We go off to the bay window and begin brainstorming. We only have two days, so we have to get this in motion right now. "Ty, since you are technical, how about you make four boxes that covers all the family and then I will put together some ornaments for each family."

"There was some plastic-ball-looking things I found in one of the closets. We need string, and what can we make the boxes with?" Ty says.

"There is some really big cardboard I can structure up, and we put the ornaments in there."

We break up to go find all our materials. We come back together and get to work. We are gluing and trying to make all kinds of stuff happen. Ty is always good with making paper mache. As he is shaping the ideas I have for the families, I begin to get colors and markers because that's all they have in the cabin. I look at everything in my hand and say to myself, *Just going to have to make it work.*

Meanwhile, the adults are walking through, acting like they're watching and seeing what our task are, but we know they're being nosy. Joz and Teli are in the living area since they insisted that they needed more space. What they had come up with was so cool. They had frames that they were making out of a collage of photos of everyone. Now I don't know how they are going to get it done, but I bet they do. The idea and concept is amazing.

We break for some lunch, and I look over at Má. She still has the same down look on her face like when I was up in the room talking to her. I go over, placing my arm around her shoulder. "You really missing Dad, huh?"

She looks up at me and smile. "Yes, I do, but he will be here before Christmas." But there is a look on her face of uncertainty. I don't press on her about the look.

I say as happily as I can, "Then before Christmas, he will be here."

As we go back to working on our projects, the adults are chilling. From all the chatter about the albums, the moms are getting ideas for Christmas dinner as they laugh and talk about memories. The dads are playing dominos without a care in the world. Mr. John gets a buzz on his phone, and the TV pops onto a game. The men are living the life.

In the middle of the game, and they are still playing dominos, there is the doorbell. We must not have heard it at first because all of a sudden, it just keeps ringing Mr. Fisher goes to the door, opens it up, pats whoever on the shoulder, and says, "Now that's how you do it." All I can see is a figure making his way to the kitchen. Then I hear Má scream. I smile, drop everything, and just as I thought, *Yep, must be Dad.* He handed Má some flowers. She grabs them and says they are her favorite. Má lights up like a Christmas tree. After they embraced each other and kissed, Dad went in where the men were to get into both games. I look back at Má and the other moms; they are giddy like little teenagers.

As I lie down to sleep, I hear "Silent Night" by the Temptations. Around here, you get the oldies played all night and all Christmas day.

I woke up to this Christmas song by a young Vanilla Wafer. I love Christmas. Christmas day, just the smell you get and the feeling of love going around everywhere. People are nicer around Christmas time—well, most of them. I head downstairs to the smell of fresh breakfast. You would think that everyone was in competition mood, but they weren't. It was just a great vibe, a great atmosphere. It was just a warmth of love, laughter, fun, and togetherness. As we are all still in our pj's eating breakfast, I'm so full of excitement because I want to see what Joz and Teli came up with, but I also want to see the parents' faces once we show them what we have worked on. Má must have seen the excitement and anticipation because she whispered in my ear, "In due time," with a smile.

As we move to the living area, I'm still holding in all my excitement. But its game time, so let's go. Ty walks around and hands everyone their boxes. The parents share, then he gives one to Teli and then to Joz. The look on their faces is priceless. As they begin to open the velvet blue box with silver writing of their name, this paper shape of what we think of most of them pops out. The paper has hardened because we soaked it in glue. Ty's parents had the shape of two doves since they have been flying the world in full sync. My parents had the military eagle with our faces on its belly. The Fishers had a book with small writing to describe their love. Mr. John had a basketball with his hand and Teli's hand holding it. Teli had a silver basketball with his favorite number on it. Joz had a camera silver since she wants to be a reporter. Everyone faces just lit up.

Then it's Joz and Teli turn, They gave everyone pic frames with some bling on it from pics of our time here together. As we all look at the pic and someone asks when, where, and how did she get these pic, she replies back "I don't ever reveal my source. Secret." We all laugh with so much cheer. The photo captured us in most unique ways. She captures the parents on the ski slopes, playing card and dominos. The pic was in black-and-white background, but the persons she gave it to was in color. Now she did some filtering for sure. For mine, she had Ty and I going around my frame, so I didn't have as much bling with myself and her and Lee in the middle. I looked a little harder, and it also had the twins and Teli in the pic too. Oh yeah, she done this all right. Ty had pic of everyone, but then going around his frame, she add some of the pics of him at the robot competition.

"Wow!" I said out loud. "We have really outdone ourselves."

"Yes, y'all have," Mr. John says as he is wiping something from his eyes.

Teli pops his shoulder. "Pa, is that a tear I see?"

"Naw just got something in my eye."

"Yeah, right man," Sr. says, and we all just laugh.

For the rest of the day, we sit around doing everything and doing nothing. Later after dinner, we sit around the fireplace, listening to the parents' talk and stories as we play cards. Joz is on her phone doing something who knows, and Teli is snacking, with crumbs falling everywhere, even some left on his mouth. LOL. The fire is getting dim, so everyone goes to their rooms. Not me. I sit on the couch and just watch the fire.

"You coming?" Joz asked.

"Not right now. I'm just going to chill a bit," I say.

"Me too." She sits next to me, not looking up from her phone.

The next morning, the day after Christmas, it is. I still have that Christmas feeling. There is still a bunch of snow on the ground. Don't know what the plans for everyone is. Teli and Mr. John are coming down with their luggage. I can see them as I'm yawning on the couch.

"Didn't know anyone was up," Mr. John says. "We have to go. I have a deadline that must get done."

"I don't want to go, Dad." Teli says, disappointed.

Sr. comes down the stairs. "You guys goin'?" he asks.

"Yes, I have a deadline," Mr. John says.

"That has nothing to do with me." Teli persists as he reaches for his luggage.

"We have plenty of room in the truck. If you don't mind, John, we can bring Teli back with us."

Mr. John looks over at Sr. and then at Teli. "Man, you sure?" Mr. John asked.

Sr. says, "Yelp."

Teli tries to hide his smile, but I see it coming. Mr. John says, "Thanks. Teli, be on your best behavior. See you in a couple of days." They hug, then fist bump, chest bump, with a pat on the back. He waves bye to me then heads out the door. Seems to me he was excited to go. Being the seventh wheel is not cool. Deadline, you come just in time.

Teli heads back upstairs with his luggage. As Sr. makes his way to the kitchen, here comes Mr. Fisher and my dad. I think to myself they are about to throw down in the kitchen. I get up from the couch and grab my cover, but it's not coming up easy as it should. I look down, and there is Joz just drooling. I leave the cover on her head, went upstairs to wash my teeth and brush my face. There's that backward talking again.

As I head down, I hear all the convo from the kitchen. Sr. has filled everyone in about Mr. John.

"You know the real reason why he left," Mr. Fisher says.

"He told Sr. Why?" Dad says as he sips his coffee.

"Naw, man, he left because he didn't have no one to be with. It's nice and all kicking with us, but it's also no fun we all can't get none." Then I hear a bunch of laughter, don't know what was so funny.

As I get to the bottom step, Ty says, "Good morning," as he passes me up to head the kitchen to eat. "Morning," I say. Joz finally pops up as she hears the laughter and smacking of the lips 'cause the breakfast is so good.

After breakfast, we all get dressed warmly, I might add, and head out to a winter botanical gardens. I've never been to one, but it sounds cold and fun. Once we arrive, even before we park, you can see really high flower displays.

"This isn't another competition, is it?" Joz asked.

"No just watch," Ty says.

"She going to have to put that phone down to do that." Teli taps Ty's shoulder with laughter.

"Hush up!" Joz snaps. "I'm going to take pic with my phone. Mind your buziness." She looks down at her phone.

I roll up on her and whisper in her ear, "You are his buziness." She looks at me with a smile as we all head into the garden.

As you walk in, there are all different kinds of flowers covered in frost. Some even have icicles hanging from them. Never seen anything like this before in my life. This is the first time I have ever been to a winter botanical gardens.

As you walk through, they describe each flower to you and when it was planted and where it is from. In some of the areas, you could hear the birds chirping. We sit on a bench outside, had some hot chocolate. From where we sat, you would have thought it was the best seat in the gardens. You could see almost everything and everyone. There is a roasted peanut, hot cocoa of all kinds, and food stands, just to name a few.

I must have been so engulfed with people-watching that I didn't notice Ty was standing in front of me with a frosted lily in a plastic protective case. "Thank you," I say as I grab for the lily.

"You are so welcome," he says as he sits back besides me."

"This is really exciting and a bunch of fun." I look at Ty and take another sip of hot chocolate, which warms my insides just right.

"I told ya you would enjoy coming down on vacay." He smiles.

"Yeah, you did."

Joz and Teli walks up, and by this time, we all realize that the sun has gone down, and it is getting dark. We go meet the parents. As we are walking, everything on the gardens begin to light up. Even the direction we are walking in, as you step, different types of flowers bloom and twirl into different colors. How cool is this. We walk under a bridge-like piece that has vines in them, but since I'm one to touch, some leaves began to light up as I touch them.

You can hear music playing, and everyone is having a great time. We get to the parents. They are sitting on blankets, and you remember earlier I told you about the birds chirping. They are mechanical birds made to fly around with bold red, green, orange, and silver on their wings. We all take a blanket, sit down, and enjoy the light show. They had all kinds of lights and animals lit up. They had people on trains, even dancing, in the garden. The conductor got off the train and talked about the history of the garden and about the light show and for us to please make a donation. As he was speaking, I was thinking to myself, *Má's already done that.* That's where you always find a way to give back. Even though it was cold, with all the excitement and activities going on, you only really felt it on your face, me mostly on my nose. I probably looked like Rudolph, I laugh to myself.

As the parade come to an end, we all head to the SUV's to the cabin. Come to think of it—we had been at the gardens all day, but a well-spent day it was.

It was the last and final day before we head home tomorrow. Gingerbread competition, come on. As I make my way down the stairs, there are three tables filled with gingerbread-house parts, jellybeans, icing of all colors, peppermints, Twizzles, gum drops, sprinkles, Tootsie Roll, and the list goes on and on. Not too long before I get to the table, I hear footsteps at the stairs, and now the gang is all here.

We all began to get our pieces and started building. I wanted to be different and extra, so I build mine open so you can see into every room—yes, two stories, of course. I even have a pool area that I did with light and dark-blue crackling-hard candy and the yard in the front with trees with powder sugar on them. I tried to put a car in the driveway, but yeah, neither worked out so I just have a nice yard.

As we are putting our houses together, everyone is working so cheerfully. I look around, and I think I really don't want any of this to end. But I know tomorrow we will all have to head out to our homes. But we will see each other again because Má and Dad are having a New Year's Day party at the house, which they do every year. So leaving here on the thirtieth gives plenty of time, as Má says, to get things done. As we say good-bye from the cabin, it's as if we all are not like right close to each other when we get home.

We walk in the house and begin to get things ready for the New Year party. We were supposed to stay at the cabin to bring in the New Year, but hey, thangs got changed. We began to decorate. We had New Year hats, accessories, and toys laid out everywhere for people to grab. The house is fully decorated from the front yard, through to the house, then to the backyard. Dad says we get to pop firecrackers and have a fireworks show. He looks like a kid in a toy store. The difference in bringing in the New Year, we usually bring it in at church, but Má wanted to do things a little different. Lee is back from Hawaii, so she will be here.

All the usuals are starting to show up, as they have food, drinks, and whatever else they can carry in with them. Maybe an hour or so into the party, right before the clock hits twelve midnight, Mz. Cy'Queita and the twins walk through the door. I must have jumped out my skin and back in again. I get all extra loud jumping up and down, running over to the twins, hugging them, and they both just give me little pats. I know they missed me—may not have been as much as I missed Shará because we are closer than Shareé and me, but they missed me.

We all head out to the backyard. Mz. Cy'Queita winks at me and says, "We are only back for a couple of days. There was no way I was missing bringing in the New Year with you guys." I just smile.

Dad has the backyard all set up. We all do the countdown. "Three, two, one!" and the fireworks go off. Everyone looks at each other with cheer, smiles, and relief because we all made it to another year.

The gang all come together with our arms around each other's shoulders, and as we all get in close so Mr. Fisher can take our pic, I say, "The gang is all back together!"

Everyone says, "Yelp!" and we break free, getting captured with plenty of laughter and smiles.

## ABOUT THE AUTHOR

I'M A WOMAN, WIFE, and mother. To be able to reach people through my writing amazes me. I have been writing poems since high school. I decided to challenge myself and see if I could write a novel. So here we go! I love to write—it's an outlet for me that I love to do on a daily. A little secret to know about me: I always dance everywhere and anywhere with or without music.